"Would you marry me?"

"Oh, I don't think so," Clarissa said matter-of-factly.

"But you love kids and you want to be married. What else is there?"

"Love. That's the real thing that holds marriages together. I believe in the power of love to change people, to change lives."

Wade nodded slowly, visualizing the children in ten years. "I believe your love could transform those children into even better adults. You're a very beautiful woman, Clarissa. When you relax, your natural beauty shines through. That's why the kids latched on to you so quick. They're good judges of character."

"All right, Wade. I will marry you for the children."

Wade sighed his relief, stood and drew her up to stand beside him. In the dim light she looked soft, vulnerable and lonely.

"No, that isn't quite right." He shook his head. "Not just for the children. For us, too. We'll make something good of this marriage, Clarissa. I promise you that."

Books by Lois Richer

Love Inspired

A Will and a Wedding #8
†*Faithfully Yours* #15
†*A Hopeful Heart* #23
†*Sweet Charity* #32
A Home, a Heart, a Husband #50
This Child of Mine #59
Baby on the Way #73
Daddy on the Way #79
Wedding on the Way #85
‡*Mother's Day Miracle* #101

†Faith, Hope & Charity
*Brides of the Seasons
‡If Wishes Were Weddings

LOIS RICHER

lives in a small Canadian prairie town with her husband, who, she says, is a "wanna-be farmer." She began writing in self-defense, as a way to escape. She says, "Come spring, tomato plants take over my flower beds, no matter how many I 'accidentally' pull up or 'prune.' By summer I'm fielding phone calls from neighbors who don't need tomatoes this fall. Come September, no one visits us, and anyone who gallantly offers to take a box invariably ends up with six. I have more recipes with tomatoes than with chocolate. Thank goodness for writing! Imaginary people with imaginary gardens are much easier to deal with!"

Lois is pleased to present this book in her new series, IF WISHES WERE WEDDINGS, for the Steeple Hill Love Inspired line. Please feel free to contact Lois at: Box 639, Nipawin, Saskatchewan, Canada S0E 1E0.

Mother's Day Miracle
Lois Richer

Love Inspired®

Published by Steeple Hill Books™

STEEPLE HILL BOOKS

ISBN 0-373-87107-4

MOTHER'S DAY MIRACLE

Copyright © 2000 by Lois Richer

Printed in U.S.A.

For I am convinced that neither death, nor life, nor angels, nor principalities, nor things present, nor things to come, nor powers, nor height, nor depth, nor any other created thing shall be able to separate us from the love of God.

—*Romans* 8:38-39

To my friend and fellow writer Lyn Cote, who is ever and always willing to help out, coerce, cajole, push, encourage and generally mother or bully me, as the situation requires, into getting the job done. From one rebel to another, thanks, chum.

Chapter One

"**D**ear God, I wish You'd send me a husband—"

Clarissa Cartwright chewed on her lower lip as the words echoed around the empty library. The patrons were gone now, trickling away one by one, hurrying toward family and home. She could imagine them gathered around the dinner table, laughing as they shared the day's events with their dear ones, making plans to sample the sweet-scented spring evening with that one special person who made your heart thump in anticipation.

Clarissa sat alone, her heart longing to be included, to be part of something. To be needed.

She tried to formulate the petition in her mind, to choose just the right words so God would understand how deeply the ache went. It wasn't hard to say it out loud. She'd been turning the words around in her heart in a silent prayer for ages, even more frequently since her cousin's Hawaiian wedding two weeks ago.

But here in the Waseka, Missouri, town library,

alone among the books she'd cared for these past ten years, Clarissa felt strangely comfortable about voicing her request to the One who'd promised to answer.

"I didn't want to be a burden, Lord, as I was growing up. But I'm an adult now, and I'd really like to be a wife." She hesitated, then breathed out the rest of it. "I want to be a mother."

It sounded like such a big request, so demanding. She hurried on to quantify it, make it easier for God to fulfil. "He doesn't have to be rich. Or even handsome."

That sounded desperate. And she wasn't. Just lonely.

"But not just any husband," she modified, staring at the stained and peeling plaster ceiling as she spoke. "A man I can love with all my heart. A man who doesn't care that I'm not young and gorgeous with lots of money, or smart, and upwardly mobile. What I really want is a man who wants to settle down and have a family. I'm so tired of being alone."

Was that everything?

Clarissa tried to get her mind off chubby babies with rosy cheeks and fisted hands. It wasn't easy. Lately she dreamed of babies all the time. She thrust the bundles of joy out of her mind. But her replacement vision of glistening white tulle over satin and lace didn't help matters in the least. Clarissa twisted her homemade flowered cotton skirt between her fingers, scrunching her eyes up as tightly as she dared.

"Could You please send a man who will love me?" she whispered, whooshing the words out on a wish and a prayer.

"Excuse me?"

Clarissa opened her eyes so fast she saw stars. A man stood at her counter. A big man. He had the kind of straight black glossy hair that hung over his collar as if he hadn't had time to get it cut. His eyes burned a deep rich chocolate in a face full of angles and planes. His lashes were—

"Excuse me, miss?" He cleared his throat and frowned at her. "Can you help me?"

Could God answer this fast? Clarissa dismissed the question almost as quickly as it entered her brain. Of course He could. He was God!

She swallowed down her surprise and nodded. "Uh-huh."

"Oh." He looked as if he wasn't sure she was telling the truth. But when a quick glance around assured him there was no one else lurking nearby he shrugged. "I'm looking for some books on birds. They're for my ne—son."

He had a son. He was married. Her hopes dashed to the worn marble floor. It was all a mistake. A silly, childish mistake. This man wasn't for her.

"Miss?"

"Yes. Yes, I heard you. I'm just thinking." She pretended she needed time to recall that section eight held most of her books on bird-watching. "What kind of birds?"

His eyebrows rose. "What kind? I don't know." His brow furrowed, then he shrugged defensively. "The kind that fly, I guess. Just birds, that's all."

Clarissa smiled, rose from her perch behind the big oak desk and clambered awkwardly down stairs that normally gave her no problem whatsoever. "I'll show you," she offered and led the way.

The nature section was only two rows over. Clarissa stopped in front of it, considered the contents, then pulled out several of the largest picture books.

"Depending on how old he is, he might like these. They have wonderful illustrations." She opened it to show him the gorgeous colors of a parrot, and then flushed with embarrassment as the hardcover tumbled to the floor.

It was a good thing the kindergarten class wasn't here to see this. Her cast-iron rule about respecting books would be open to criticism by those curious five-year-olds.

"I'm sorry," she murmured when he handed it back.

"It's okay. Actually, I should have been clearer. I'm looking for something that would show some birds native to the area. Pierce is doing a project for school."

He tossed back his hair, raking through it with one hand. Clarissa caught the fresh clean scent of soap and smiled. She liked a man who didn't pour overpowering cologne all over himself.

You have no business liking this one, her conscience reminded. He's married. With a son.

"Feel free to look through any of these then. Maybe you'll find something you like."

She stepped back, indicating the shelf. When he bent to peer at the titles without answering her, Clarissa decided his actions spoke louder than words. He hadn't even noticed her. And why would he? Nobody noticed Clarissa. She'd become a fixture around here.

Why, I doubt anyone even noticed I've been gone, she told herself sternly. It wasn't as if she had a tan to show for her vacation in Hawaii. Her skin was too fair to do anything but burn an ugly beet red that peeled in the most unbecoming way, and she'd prevented that with liberal amounts of sunblock.

Turning with a sigh, she walked slowly back up to her desk and began tallying the column titled "Lent for the Day."

"I'll take these. If you don't mind, that is. I don't have a card." He held out four of the biggest books hesitantly. "Is that too many?"

"Certainly not. And I can make a card up for you right now. Name please?" She smiled and pulled an application form over, her pen poised to record the necessary statistics.

"Wade Featherhawk. Box 692. Telephone…"

He listed the information rapidly. Clarissa had to write quickly to get it all down.

"Good." She picked up the card and leaflet and handed them over. "The books are due in two weeks. The library hours are posted inside the leaflet, but you can always slip the books through the slot if it's after hours. By the way, I'm Clarissa Cartwright." She held out her hand.

Stark, utter silence greeted her announcement. The brown-black eyes that twinkled mere moments ago now frosted over. His hand, halfway up, dropped back down by his side.

"Oh." He took the books from her carefully, making sure that their fingers had no contact. "I, uh, I should probably tell you right off that I'm not interested."

"I beg your pardon?" Clarissa frowned, glancing

at the clock. She was two minutes late closing. Hm, according to Hawaii time, that was...

"I'm not looking for a wife." The blunt-edged words came from lips stretched in a thin line of animosity. "I can handle the kids myself. I don't need somebody tagging around after me, nagging me to do this or that. I can manage my life just fine."

Clarissa froze. Surely he hadn't heard her praying? Her face heated at the worried look in his eye. She licked her lips and stuttered out a response.

"I—I d-don't know what you mean. I have never—"

"Look, I probably shouldn't have said anything. It's just that Norman Paisley told me about you being single and all. Then Mrs. Nettles expounded on your assets as the perfect wife. After that a lady I've never met before told me how great you are at caring for people. In fact, that's all I've heard for the past week."

He didn't sound exactly thrilled with what he learned either, Clarissa decided grimly.

She shook with the sheer humiliation of it. They were trying to marry her off again! And to the first available man who stepped into town. The heat of embarrassment clawed up her neck and flooded her face. Desperately she searched for composure while praying that he hadn't heard her prayer.

"I'm so sorry!" She flushed again at his disparaging look and searched for the shortest possible explanation. "I was orphaned when I was young. My parents worked overseas, and I was too much of a burden. My Gran raised me. Along with half the town. They feel responsible, sort of a community of adopted parents. They're kind of…well, rather like a big, nosy family.'' Clarissa gulped, knowing she was babbling, but unable to stop.

"I've been away, you see. On vacation. I didn't realize…''

She made herself stop at the less than spellbound look on his face. It was obvious he couldn't care less. He shifted from one foot to the other in patent disinterest, politely waiting for her to stop speaking.

"Well, I just wanted to warn you that I'm not in the market.'' His lips pinched tight as he glared at her. It was obvious that he hated having to spell it out.

Only when she peered into his eyes did Clarissa catch a hint of the suspicion in his eyes. Wariness. As if he were waiting. But for what? Clarissa mustered her composure, straightened her spine and smiled cooly.

"I'm sorry you felt you had to defend yourself, Mr. Featherhawk. I've lived here all of my life, and the people here tend to think of me as their responsibility. Rest assured, I have no intention of chasing you. In spite of what they told you, I don't need a husband that badly.''

"Sorry. My mistake.'' He frowned as if he didn't quite believe her, but was prepared to accept it just the same. "No problem.''

The odd look he cast over her made her wonder if he hadn't heard every word of her desperately uttered prayer, but Clarissa refused to speculate. It was done. She couldn't change anything. Far better to keep her pride intact and pretend nothing untoward had happened here this afternoon. There would be time enough to cry over spilled milk later, at home, alone.

"The library will be closing in just a few minutes. Is there anything else I can help you with?" She kept her friendly smile in place through sheer perversity, merely nodding when he shook his head. "Fine. Have a good day."

"You, too," he mumbled before striding across the room and out the door.

As the heavy oak banged shut behind him, Clarissa heaved a sigh of relief mingled with regret. He was so handsome!

"Okay, God. I get the message. You're in control. You'll decide when and if I should get married, let alone be a mother." She closed and locked the fine drawer, which never held more than three dollars anyway, placed her pen in the holder and pushed her chair neatly behind the big desk.

"It's in Your hands," she acquiesced with a sigh. "But I'm not getting any younger. I hope You keep in mind that I'm no spring chicken, and I would like to enjoy my kids while I'm still young enough to keep up with them. If I get kids, that is."

Since there was no audible reply, or any other sign from above, Clarissa picked up the sweater she'd worn this morning, grabbed her handbag and her empty lunch sack and walked out of the musty building. It took only a second to lock the solid worn door.

Clarissa trod down the steps carefully, grateful for the fresh late-afternoon breeze that still blew. She needed a little air after her first day back at work.

A busy little town that drew on the agricultural industry surrounding it, Waseka hummed with early springtime activity. The place was so small that everybody knew everybody else, and their business. Which was part of Clarissa's problem, but also part of the reason she loved it here.

It meant that they all knew how Harrison Harder had abandoned her the day before her wedding, to marry that city upstart who'd only been back in town for three weeks and claimed to be Clarissa's best friend. Today the reminder of his defection only made her smile.

Harrison Harder! The same man who'd trailed after her since seventh grade, defended her from Tommy Cummings when she hadn't needed his help, and vowed that he'd never love anyone else.

Clarissa had smiled her way through those awful days, too. The nights she spent weeping for a precious dream that had died. It was then that she'd realized that Harrison had only been the means to an end. Now she wasn't sure she'd ever *really* loved him, not the way a wife needed to love her husband. He'd been her way of getting the family she craved, of avoiding having to move in with one of the greataunts just for company.

Her minister had tried to counsel her, to tell her that sometimes God sent roadblocks so people could see they were going down the wrong path. He was staunch in his belief that God had something much better in store for her. Clarissa tried to accept that, but with every day that passed, all she felt was more empty, more alone, more of an outsider in a town where everyone had someone.

That solitary feeling magnified when Gran died three years ago and Clarissa was left with a big, old house, and a hole in her heart. Who would she love now? Would she never have the family she'd longed for ever since her parents had died?

But all that was years ago. Clarissa didn't have any tears left for Harrison. Instead, she stubbornly clung to her dream. A family, a big, happy family where she showered all the devotion she wanted on people who would reciprocate with enough to fill her needy heart.

She ached for her own circle of love, especially now, after that wedding in Hawaii where honeymoon couples abounded. In fact, the surfeit of amorous couples found at those weddings was a perfectly good reason for avoiding the next one!

"Hi, Clarissa. Noticed you met our newest resident." Millie Perkins giggled, her broad face wreathed in smiles. "Now there's a fine specimen of a man. He'd make a good husband for you. And is he handsome!"

"You mean Wade Featherhawk? Yes, I met him." Clarissa blushed, recalling that prayer. "I don't think he's interested in me, Millie." Belatedly she remembered he was married.

"Nonsense! Of course he's interested. Just doesn't want to seem too eager is all. A man in his condition needs a good woman." Millie thumped her purse as if that settled the matter.

In his condition? Clarissa's radar went on high alert. She didn't want to fix anyone else's problems. She'd had enough of that with Billy Stuart and Lester Short, two men she'd once agreed to date. She still regretted those hastily made encounters.

"He said he was looking for a book for his son."

Clarissa half-whispered it, wondering how long it would take the older woman to spill the beans she was obviously so anxious to share.

The day had been long. Clarissa was tired and hungry and she wanted to go home. She wouldn't tell a soul that what she really wanted was to spend some time thinking about that tall, dark man she'd met this afternoon. Instead, she prepared to hear the local's lowdown on one Wade Featherhawk.

"You've been away so I'll fill you in. Came to town the day after you left. Seems Jerry Crane is a friend of his, and Wade put a bid in on that country club Jerry's building." Millie stopped just long enough to gulp for air. "Jerry announced the winners last week, and first thing you know we have a new resident." She nodded smugly, as if she'd done her share of arranging that.

"So he's a carpenter. That's nice." Clarissa pushed away the thought of those big, rough hands.

"Apparently a good one, too. Or so Jerry says." Millie huffed once more and continued. "He didn't come alone. No, sir. He's got a passel of kids. Not his, though. And no wife. Myrna Mahoney over at Sally's Café told me that. The bunch of 'em were living at the motel for a while. Must have been terrible expensive. Heard they moved. She couldn't find out where. He doesn't talk much. The strong, silent type."

Millie hitched up her purse, adjusted the snug skirt surrounding her burgeoning hips and shoved her hat farther down on her freshly permed hair. "I've gotta go, hon. Burt doesn't like for me to be away too long when they're seeding."

"Yes, of course. Bye, Millie." Clarissa, embarrassed to find herself so interested in a perfect stranger, waved politely and started toward home once more, quickly jaywalking across to the fire hall to avoid Betty Fields, whom she saw waiting on the next corner.

She opened the white picket gate that led to her yard and stepped inside, appreciating the lovely old house as she went.

"It needs a coat of paint and some work on the roof, but it's still a great house," she assured herself. "A perfect house for a family. With a little work."

Dinner didn't take long. She'd set out her pork chop to thaw that morning. As she waited for her potato to boil, she wished again for a microwave. Better yet, a family to cook for! Making food for one was so boring. Baking one potato in the oven meant heating up the whole house, and it seemed foolish to do that with electricity so high. As she pulled a bottle of blue cheese dressing out of the fridge, she caught sight of the chocolate Valentine she'd given herself.

"Should have thrown that out." Instead, she closed the door on it, just as she'd shut down her hopes and dreams. There was no point wishing for something that was never going to happen.

Since it was still light outside after her meal and the silence inside the house was somehow depressing, Clarissa decided to finish working her flower bed. She'd always been one of the first to have pansies and petunias blooming. This year wouldn't be any different.

It is a silly dream, she lectured herself, kneeling to insert the delicate bedding plants. *Lots of people would say I'm too old to keep daydreaming about kids. Even if I had a husband who wanted them. Which I don't.*

She sighed at the hopelessness of it all and transplanted another flat of flowers.

"Can I see your birds?" A little boy with freckles on his nose and a spot of dirt on his cheek, peered through the pickets of her backyard fence. "They're goldfinches, aren't they?"

Clarissa thrust the dream of cherubic babies out of her mind and stared at the chubby little boy who stood impatiently waiting to enter her yard.

"No one ever uses that gate," she murmured, frowning. "I keep it oiled, of course. But still, it's very difficult to open."

"I can climb over." In a matter of seconds the little boy hiked himself over the fence. He stood before her, panting as he studied her birds. One bit of his jeans still clung to the top of the fence, but he ignored that. "How many do you got?"

"What? Oh, the birds. I'm not sure. Eight, I think. I don't keep them caged, but they always come here for the seeds."

"That's 'cause they like livin' in the woods over there." The child inclined his head to the wild growth of trees and shrubs that occupied the land next to hers. "Finches prefer to build their nests in low bushes or trees."

"I expect so." She studied him. He was a curious blend. A child, yes, but with intelligent eyes and an obvious thirst for knowledge. She remembered the man at the library. "Do you like birds?" she asked curiously.

"Oh, yes!" His face was a delight to watch, eyes shining, mouth stretched wide in a smile of pure bliss. "I collect pictures of them." He flopped down on the grass beside her and opened the pad he carried. Inside he'd detailed a carefully organized listing of birds he'd seen, with the odd picture taped here and there. "What's your name?"

"Clarissa Cartwright," she told him smiling. "And yours?"

"Pete. Do you have any cookies?" His look beseeched her to say yes. "I sure am hungry."

He couldn't have known that was the path straight to her heart, Clarissa decided. He couldn't possibly know how much she longed to share her special double fudge nut chip cookies with a child who would appreciate the thick chocolate chunks.

"As a matter of fact, I do have cookies. Would you like some?"

He nodded vehemently. "I'm starved! I didn't eat nothin' for supper."

"Why ever not?" She frowned. Children needed good nourishing food. His parents should be more careful. She wondered who they were.

"Supper didn't taste so good. Tildy made it an' she burns a lot of stuff." He glanced behind quickly, then lowered his voice. "But I'm not s'posed to say nothin' so's I don't hurt her feelings."

"That's very kind of you." Clarissa got to her feet, happy to leave the planting if it meant sharing her cookies. "I'll bring some milk out too, shall I?"

He trailed along behind her, up the stairs and in through the back door, with nary a hint of indecision.

"Do you live here all by yourself?" he asked, his face filled with curiosity as he looked around.

"Mm-hm. It was my grandmother's house. She left it for me to live in when she died." Clarissa set six cookies on a plate, poured two large glasses of milk, then checked to be sure Tabby the cat had some milk in her bowl. "My parents died when I was a little girl. My grandma looked after me."

"I don't gots no mother, neither." Pete took the plate and obediently carried it out onto her veranda behind her. "She died. My dad, too. Me an' my brother and my dopey sisters are the only ones left." He took a huge bite of cookie. "I'm getting 'dopted."

"That's nice." Clarissa smiled to hide the shaft of pain she felt at the sad story. "I'm sure your new parents must love you very much." She set the milk down and pulled out a chair.

"Enough to confine him to his room for a week if he doesn't learn to stay in his own yard," a husky voice informed her sardonically. "There's something wrong with your back gate."

Clarissa gasped at the familiar timbre of those low tones. She whirled around, her face draining of color as she met the dark forbidding gaze of the man who'd been in her library that very afternoon.

"What are you doing here?" she demanded, noticing that he'd left the front gate open. She hurried to close it. "I don't allow cats in my yard," she told him soberly. "They bother the birds."

"But you got a cat in your house. I seen it." Pete's shrill voice burst into the conversation.

"You 'saw' it. And Tabby doesn't go outside."

Clarissa stood where she was, her hands buried in the voluminous pockets of her long skirt. "Are you Pete's father?"

"His name is Pierce and you know very well that I'm his uncle. I'm sure the entire town has informed you of my existence by now. I have to tell you that I do not appreciate having to scour the neighborhood to find my nephew, Miss Cartwright."

"Hey, I didn't steal him!" Clarissa burst out, affronted by the implication in that low voice. "He came to look at the birds." Another thought occurred and she whirled to face Pete, who was now enjoying his fifth cookie. "Is Pierce your real name?"

"Yeah." Pierce looked shamefaced, his soft melting eyes begged forgiveness. "But I like people to call me Pete. It's not so...weird." He pocketed the last cookie, then stared up at the big man who stood towering over them both. "I'll go home now, Uncle Wade. I'm sorry I disobeyed."

Clarissa hadn't thought it possible, but the stern craggy face softened, just a little.

"It's all right this time, son. But please stay in the yard. That's why I rented the place, so there would be room for all of you to run and jump and play without getting into trouble." His uncle eyed the torn jeans with a rueful smile. "Another pair? How do you manage to do this, Pierce?"

"I dunno. It just happens." Pierce shuffled down the steps, then raced around to the back of the house for his book. "See ya later," he called to Clarissa, then vaulted over the fence with a huge leap.

"You're his *uncle?*" Somehow the knowledge just now made its way to her brain. "But this afternoon you said you were looking for a book for your son. And Pete, I mean Pierce, said he was adopted." She frowned, trying to fit it all together.

As the worst possible scenario flew into her mind, she gasped. She'd seen those milk-carton pictures for years, children who'd been stolen from one parent by another.

"You can forget whatever you're thinking. I *am* their legal guardian." His rumbly voice openly mocked her.

"They?" She pounced on the information, struggling to assimilate it all. "Who are they?"

His face twisted into a wry smile. "One of the meddlers around here really must have slipped up."

When Clarissa only frowned in perplexity, he sighed, rolled his eyes, then thrust out one hand.

"I suppose we didn't get off to a very good start. You already know my name. And yes, before you ask, I'm part Cree. On my mother's side. She kept her name." His dark fuming eyes dared her to make something of that. "My sister and her husband died and left their kids for me to look after. Tildy and Lacey are twins. They're twelve. Jared is ten and Pierce is seven. We moved here for the work. I would have thought the gossips would have imparted at least that much."

Clarissa took his hand and shook it, feeling the zap of his touch shiver all the way up her arm.

"I don't listen to gossip," she assured him in a daze.

Four children? This man was raising four children? Alone? "Welcome to Waseka." She managed to get the words out despite the shock that held her jaw tense.

"In case you didn't understand earlier, I think I should make one thing perfectly clear," he muttered, yanking his hand away and shoving it into the pocket of his worn but very well fitted jeans. "I'm not looking for a wife. Despite what people think, men are as capable of parenting as women. Nobody's going to go hungry or get abandoned or forgotten about. I promised my sister I'd care for them, and I'll keep my word. I'll do my duty. Me. By myself." His lips tightened. "In spite of the locals' opinion, I've been doing just fine for several months now. And I intend to keep it that way."

She wondered why he sounded so torn about it. Then the impact of his words hit home.

"Now, just a minute here." Clarissa felt the flush push up from her neck, right to the roots of her string-straight hair.

"No, you wait. I know what small towns are like. Nosy bunch of old fools! Everybody's been hinting about you since the day I walked into this one-horse place. 'Clarissa's a wonderful cook. Clarissa's so good with kids. Clarissa would make you the perfect wife. She just loves to care for people.' Yak, yak, yak." He snorted derisively, eyeing the plate that now held only a few crumbs. "I can see you've already been practicing your motherly wiles on my nephew."

"Wiles? I wasn't—"

"I've heard it all before, you know. Too many times. The sweet praise for a man who can care for four children. The innocent suggestion that I might need help. The generous offer to cook us a healthy meal. Out of friendship, of course! Matchmakers!'' One corner of his unsmiling mouth tipped down.

"Forget about whatever you're planning, Miss Cartwright. We're not in the market. I don't need the aggravation." Wade Featherhawk turned and stomped down the walk, his face grim and forbidding.

Clarissa followed him down, her brain working furiously. "But, wait a minute. I didn't even—"

He whirled around faster than she expected, bumping into her. One tanned hand grabbed her arm, waited until she was steady, then fell away as if it had been burned.

"No, you wait. Maybe I didn't make it clear enough. I'm not interested in whatever you're offering. My family is doing just fine. I don't need your interference." His snapping black eyes told her just how little she interested him. When Clarissa didn't back off, he smiled darkly.

"I don't go for blondes, and even if I did, I'd pick someone strong enough to handle four kids, not a woman who looks like she'd blow away in the first storm that came along." His eyes glinted black as ebony. "You want to mother someone, *Miss* Cartwright? Find your own kids."

Clarissa cringed away from him, but she refused to allow him to get away with saying such things to her. Whatever was behind his glowering countenance, it couldn't cover this deplorable lack of good manners.

"Believe me, Mr. Featherhawk, I wouldn't bother to give you the time of day! But I feel sorry for those children. If you're this cranky all the time, they must really bask in your company. A veritable joy to live with!''

Clarissa had never been so furious in her life. She stomped up the stairs, picked up Pierce's empty glass and plate, and stormed into the house, slamming the door behind her. As usual, the door immediately flopped open, and waved back and forth on its hinges with the annoying creak it always made when ill-treated.

A burst of laughter from outside made her flush even hotter. She slapped the dishes down and whirled back to the door to face his supercilious look.

"While you're looking for someone to share your life with, I'd make sure he knows how to build. This mausoleum is going to fall down around your ears if you don't do something soon, Miss Cartwright. Not that I'm volunteering." He frowned, took a step backward and shook his head. "No way! I'm not into masochism. Good night."

Clarissa seethed with indignation. Of all the arrogant, rude, obnoxious men, Wade Featherhawk had to take the cake. She closed the door firmly on his snide words and then wondered if he'd been referring only to the house.

The phone pealed a summons and Clarissa picked it up reluctantly. *Please Lord, not another busybody.*

"Hi, Prissy! How was Hawaii?" Her college buddy, Blair Delayney's bright voice echoed from the far reaches of the Rocky Mountains. "Meet any gorgeous men?"

"Nope, not a one. I'm still part of the group. How about you and Briony?" She wouldn't say a thing about the one who'd just left her front yard.

It was an old joke. In college, all three women had planned to be married and then lost their grooms one way or another before the ceremony. Down but not out, they'd banded together, calling themselves the Three Spinsters, vowing never to go looking for love again.

The only problem was, none of them could seem to accept in their hearts that love wouldn't find them. Someday.

"Oh, we're both still old maids. How was the wedding?" Blair always demanded details.

"It was lovely. On the beach, at sunset. That exclusive club was something else, though I felt out of place. I didn't know anyone except Great-Aunt Martha and she's deaf." Clarissa described the elegant dresses of the guests as best she could.

"I told you to take along a friend. Hawaii's a hard place to be alone." Blair's voice softened in commiseration.

"Tell me about it." Clarissa rested her cheek against the coolness of the wall. "Everywhere I went there were couples. Old ones, young ones, but always couples. Even some with kids."

"I'm sorry, Priss." Blair and Bri were the only two who knew how much she wanted to be a mother.

The old nickname came from her college days when she was constantly chiding them about cleaning up the apartment. It was somehow comforting to Clarissa. "Don't be. I managed all right once the aunt left and I got to look around on my own. There's this museum, Blair. You wouldn't believe the stuff!"

She launched into a description of the Bishop Museum that left little time for her to recount the lonely evenings spent walking along the silver-lined sand by herself, longing for someone to share all that beauty with. By the time Blair rang off, she was hooting with laughter. Which was exactly what Clarissa wanted. No one feeling sorry for her.

She rinsed off the dishes and stacked them in the cavernous dishwasher, empty except for her dinner plate and cutlery. She considered Wade's stinging assessment as she worked. Her lips pinched tight in anger as she remembered Pierce's yearning look at the pie she'd made for Mr. Harper.

"We'll see who has the last laugh, Mr. Wade Featherhawk. We'll just see. I wouldn't offer to help you if you begged me on bended knee!"

The mental picture this brought to mind made her burst out laughing. Wade Featherhawk, on his knees, to her?

"In your dreams, woman." She giggled out loud. She'd often dreamed of being proposed to, but it wasn't going to happen this time either, prayer notwithstanding. "Just forget about him."

If only it was that easy.

Chapter Two

Two weeks later Wade glanced around the old-fashioned church and grimaced as he caught sight of Clarissa Cartwright's willowy figure two pews ahead. Her dainty blue-and-white-flowered dress accentuated her gorgeous blond hair and the narrowness of her waist, along with other assets he forbade himself to notice. She was tiny. As he studied her clear profile and smooth white skin, his body tensed, his hands clenched and his jaw tightened. Wade told himself it was anger.

Everywhere he went these days, *she* seemed to be there, waiting in the wings, a silent reminder that he wasn't a very good father, that he didn't know diddly about parenting. That duty and obligation were no substitute for the mother's love that the kids needed.

She never said a word, of course, but he knew she was inaudibly pointing out the fact that he didn't have a clue as to what he was doing when it came to raising kids, especially girls.

Just his luck that Tildy and Lacey had Clarissa for a Sunday school teacher, Jared drew her as his special pal in Boys' Club, and Pierce couldn't stop singing the praises of her dim, moldy old library. Some luck, Wade decided grimly.

No sooner was Wade's back turned than Clarissa invited one or the other of them over to that mausoleum. For a snack, to plan an outing, to practice a new recipe. Blah, blah, blah.

Wade was fed up to the teeth hearing about Miss Clarissa Cartwright and her wonderful life! All it did was make him look incompetent and lacking. Which he was! But he didn't need it rubbed in.

"Good to see you here." A man whose name Wade couldn't remember pumped his hand up and down, his face beaming. "Glad to have you in Waseka."

"Uh, thanks." Wade felt vaguely ashamed of his churlish behavior. Not everyone was all bad.

"You ever bowl? We're one short on our team and I sure wouldn't mind getting someone who can roll a few strikes. Call me up if you're interested. Ed Mason's the name."

"Thanks. I don't have a lot of free time, but I'll think about it." Wade watched the other man saunter away, then turned to gather his brood. Instead, he found himself virtually alone inside the building. Now what?

He sauntered down the aisle and out the door. They were there on the lawn, all four of them, clustered around *her*, laughing and giggling. Probably at some remark she'd made about him. Wade felt his jaw tighten in annoyance and struggled to suppress it. Why did she get under his skin like this?

"Really? A picnic? What would we have?" That was Jared, consumed with the condition of his perpetually empty stomach.

"Mm, fried chicken, maybe? With potato salad. And watermelon scones." Clarissa brushed a hand over Tildy's riot of inexpertly permed curls. "Maybe some chocolate layer cake for dessert. Or strawberry shortcake. How does that sound?"

"Like I died and went to heaven." Jared groaned, patting his ribs. "When can we go?"

"You can't." Wade walked up behind them, frowning in reproof at Clarissa. "Miss Cartwright has other things to do. And we can manage meals perfectly well on our own."

"But Clarissa was going to teach me how to make fried chicken for my home ec class," Tildy protested. "And Lacey wants to get some help with that biology paper."

"I'll help her. And we can buy fried chicken in town. Or make it at home. Let's go." He herded them toward the sidewalk. "Tildy, you, Lacey and the boys go ahead and get lunch started. I just have to stop and talk to someone for a minute. I'll be right there."

"Yes, Uncle Wade." Tildy didn't even look at him, but he could tell from the pout on her pretty face that she wasn't happy with his edict. Her heels hit the pavement with hard, knee-jarring thumps.

Wade winced at the girl's anger while his own temper inched up another degree. It was all *her* fault! All this meddling from their nosy neighbor had made the kids rebellious. He turned back toward the church with vengeance fogging his brain.

"Miss Cartwright, I asked you to leave us alone. Why can't you respect my wishes?"

She stared at him, her eyes big pools of innocence in her long thin face.

"I didn't encourage them. Really! It was just that Pierce mentioned it was a lovely day for bird-watching. Then Jared suggested a picnic, and I joined in his game of pretend. I wasn't hinting anything."

Her face, open and oh, so innocent, peered back at him.

"Yeah, right." He led her out of the way of the crowd and off to one side. Then he stood in front of her, daring her to try to wiggle out of this one. "I'm asking you for the last time to leave my kids alone. We don't need your help. It was nice of you to do what you've done, and I do appreciate it, but we're settled in now and we're doing just fine by ourselves."

She looked a little surprised and confused by his words. That blank, credulous look made him say something he shouldn't have.

"Please, lady, just leave us alone. I know you want to help but you can't. No one can. I've got to do this on my own, no matter how much I might want somebody there to share the load. We've got to learn how to be a family together. Alone."

"I'm sorry! I didn't mean to offend you," she whispered, her face ashen. The twinkle of happiness he'd glimpsed earlier disappeared. "I just thought I could help out. I didn't think you'd find out about the jeans or the ironing."

Wade felt his face freeze. He allowed his gaze to slip just a little lower, to the pressed cotton of his shirt. He should have known Lacey hadn't done it!

"They're so busy doing chores all day, they don't have time to play. Everything is so serious for them. I was just trying to lend a hand." Her earnest voice pleaded with him to understand, dropped almost to a whisper. "I know what it's like to feel as if you have to earn your keep."

Wade felt the pain in those softly spoken words and wondered what had caused it. Clarissa Cartwright hardly looked like a little Cinderella. In spite of that, he couldn't stem the tide of chagrin that rose in a wave of gall. How dare she go to his house, check out his family and how he provided for them? How dare she snoop through his home on the pretext of mending their worn clothes? He knew they weren't the best, but at least they were clean and paid for. Well, most of the time they were clean.

"Look, maybe we don't live the kind of dream life you want. I know the kids have to pitch in. But it won't hurt them. They'll learn accountability. Raising them *is* up to me, not you." He felt a tide of red rise in his cheeks as he noticed the tiny mending stitches on the knee of his jeans.

Even in the best of all possible worlds, his nieces couldn't sew like that, and he should have known it, would have known it if he'd paid more attention to them.

"I love those kids as if they were my very own. They're not going to get mixed up in drugs or booze or any of that stuff as long as I'm around." He took a deep breath and continued. "But they're not going to have a mother, either. Not even a pretend one. And they have to face that." He took a deep breath and went on the attack.

"So I wish you'd stop trying to weasel your way into our lives just so you can prove to everyone how much better off you'd treat them. In two words, Miss Cartwright—butt out!"

Wade turned and found several pairs of eyes on him. He knew then that the congregation had heard every word he'd said. Before the noon siren screamed across the town, they'd spread it far and wide. A surge of remorse washed over him, but he thrust it away, his mind boiling with frustration.

Maybe now these people would stop shoving Clarissa Cartwright's single status in his face!

Wade made himself spend time talking with Pastor Mike, chatting to Jerry about the walk-in cedar closet he wanted in his house. By the time he strode down the sidewalk, hands clenched inside his pockets, most of the folks had dispersed. And that included Clarissa. He'd known the exact moment she'd scurried away, head downcast, shoulders slumped.

He forced his mind away off her and took a detour on the way home in order to concentrate on the list of jobs he'd garnered around town. With a little luck, maybe he could make enough to put some money in the bank for that rainy day that kept happening when work ran out. He was going to need a little extra cash. Especially now, with the country club project delayed.

It wasn't five minutes before he got caught up in studying the Victorian architecture of the row of houses on Primrose Lane. He kept walking, trying to remember the details he'd planted deep in his brain last year in order to gain acceptance to the college of architecture.

As he studied gables and turrets, Wade let his mind turn over the problem of life in Waseka. He'd tried to keep to himself, tried to avoid the inevitable matchmaking. He'd been through it enough times. And every time the kids got their hopes up, he had to dash them because the woman in question always wanted something he couldn't give. She sure wasn't looking to take on a ready-made family that belonged to someone else. At least, that's what he told himself. The truth was, he didn't want the responsibility of yet another person cluttering up his life.

Wade trudged down the street with the sun beating on his head, lost in his thoughts of providing a future for four needy children who were totally dependent on him. His shoulders bowed under all that being their parent demanded, the knowledge that he was no good at responsibility nagging in the back of his brain.

He flinched in surprise when small, sharp-nailed fingers closed around his arm, pinching tight in their effort to penetrate and thus slow him down. Wade flung the hand away, then whirled around to see who was attacking him.

She stood there, sea foam eyes turbulent with temper. Clarissa might have to look up to meet his gaze, but she certainly didn't seem intimidated. She looked more like a wasp about to sting.

"How dare you embarrass me like that? I didn't help them out because of you! I wouldn't do anything for you. You're too stubborn and far too arrogant to want to help, Mr. Featherhawk.'' Her words were so sharp, they could have torn a strip off him.

He waited, mentally flinching at the fury in her face, but keeping his own countenance impassive.

"Did I mention self-absorbed?'' She crossed both arms across her chest and glared. "Or conceited? I did it for them, you know. Because they deserve some decent food, some time to play, a clean house and a shoulder to cry on once in a while. They've had to grow up awfully fast since their parents' deaths. Can't you let them be children for even one afternoon without lording it over them and forcing them to wallow in the drudgery?''

Oh, brother! Over the past two weeks they must have poured out the whole ugly story. As if he wanted to deprive them of anything when they'd already lost both parents. Wade sighed, his whole body sagging with tiredness as she continued her diatribe. As he waited, she slapped her hands on her hips and laughed, a harsh discordant sound that didn't match her delicate looks.

"You're so worried about getting trapped—who would want to marry you anyway?'' She sniffed, her snubbed nose tipped upward in haughty reproof. "It's not as if you're the least bit *pleasant* to be around. I feel sorry for those kids, living with a bear like you, Wade Featherhawk. You carry a chip big enough for the whole Cree nation.''

Clarissa gave him one last huff, then turned and stomped away, her heels tap-tapping on the sidewalk. Openmouthed, Wade watched her until she closed her white picket gate, climbed the steps to her rickety old house and firmly closed the door on him. He shook his head to clear it, wondering why he'd chosen this street anyway.

Then he turned the corner toward home, his shoulders hunching forward as he thought over what she'd said.

"Way to go, bud! You've already got so many friends in this place, you can really afford to slap down the one person who was willing to help out, no questions asked. Smart, very smart."

He shut his mind on that mocking inner voice and kept walking toward the park. He needed to think....

Wade wasn't sure how much time passed before he wandered out of the park and down the street. He scanned the sky, but that didn't help. Heritage or not, he couldn't tell time by the sun. His eyes narrowed as he focused on the plume of smoke coming from down the street. From his house! Wade broke into a sprint that carried him through the front door and into the kitchen in less than a minute.

"Tildy? Something's burning." He grabbed a pot mitt and lifted the smoke-belching pan from the stove, searching for a place to set it down.

Since the counter was covered with dirty dishes and the table still held the remains of breakfast, he carried the pot outside and across the backyard to dump its charred remains into the garbage barrel.

Clarissa Cartwright stood across the alley, in her own yard, fork poised over a barbeque. She raised one eyebrow quizzically.

"Problem?" she enquired softly, glancing down at the pot.

"Not at all," he lied.

"Oh, good. Well, if the children want to accept my invitation, I have extra steaks in the fridge and lots of potatoes right here, ready to roast. There's apple pie for dessert and I made fresh lemonade. *They're* more than welcome."

Meaning he wasn't? Wade sighed. No question about it. He'd burned his bridges there. She'd probably cross the street to avoid him from now on. But that was what he'd wanted, wasn't it?

She turned the item on her barbeque and Wade felt his mouth water, his tongue prickle, his stomach rumble. A T-bone steak! What he wouldn't give for a nice juicy steak on the rare side with a fluffy baked potato heaping with sour cream. And a slice of apple pie.

He closed his eyes and gulped, swallowing the gall that rose in his throat as he humbly ate crow. You didn't take someone up on an invitation like that after you'd embarrassed them in front of half the town.

"Th-thanks anyway. But we've got our dinner ready." He wished he could chuck the pot into the garbage can, too. It would take forever to clean.

"Yes, I can see that." She gave him one last questioning look, then turned her back and lifted a sizzling steak from the grill, watching as the juices dripped onto the coals. "A little too rare, I think." She laid it back down.

Wade swallowed again, scraped what he could out of his pot and returned to his messy, smoke-filled home with legs like cement.

As he gathered the kids around the table to munch on tasteless, white buttered bread spread with gobs of oily peanut butter, he faced the condemning looks in their eyes.

"To think we could have been eating real food. Steak," Jared grumbled, glaring at the sandwich. "And pie. I heard her from my window. Pie!"

"Know what my Sunday school lesson was about today, Uncle Wade?" Lacey's pretty face darkened like a thundercloud about to dump its contents all over him.

"I can't imagine." He chewed slowly, almost gagging when he tried to swallow the sticky concoction.

"Pride," Lacey informed him sagely. "Silly, stupid pride. It always comes before a fall."

"Oh. That's nice, dear."

A resounding silence greeted his words. Then, one by one, the kids left the table, their sandwiches torn apart, but mostly uneaten.

Wade took a gulp of water, then folded his napkin over the rest of his sandwich. He couldn't eat another bite either.

Grimly he wondered how much damage it would do to his image to admit defeat and take them all out to the fast-food place for supper. He'd almost decided to do it when he saw Pierce sneak across the backyard and vault over *her* fence.

Not two minutes later the boy was sprawled on the grass, happily munching on something, his freckled face the picture of bliss as he gazed lovingly at Wade's nemesis.

As he worked on cleaning up the kitchen, Wade had lots of time to notice that it wasn't long before Jared, followed by Tildy and Lacey, decided to go for a walk. And when Clarissa and Pierce disappeared from her backyard, he knew exactly where all three had gone.

"Bribing them," he muttered, viciously scraping last night's burnt hamburger out of the frying pan. "That's all she's doing."

His stomach rumbled agreement, and he threw down the pot scrubber in defeat.

"Sally's Café is open this afternoon. I believe I'll stop by for coffee with the boys."

Wade pulled open the door, his toe thudding against the box that sat leaning against the closet door. Why had he hung on to his drafting table anyway? It wasn't as if he'd ever realize that ambition. It was better to get rid of all the evidence of his aspirations to become an architect. Supporting four kids took every dime he made and more moments than he had in a day. Finding time to study would be impossible.

Wade picked up the box, opened the closet and stuffed it against the back wall, standing the rolls of vellum filled with his carefully sketched ideas behind the winter coats. He had only himself to blame—his sister, Kendra, would be living somewhere with her children if he hadn't insisted she give her husband another chance, try to make their marriage work. That's what had killed her and ended his dream, his insistence on avoiding his duty to her.

Wouldn't it have been better to let Kendra move out on Roy, come and live with him, instead of asking her to work things out? He'd laid it on heavy, reminded her how much the boys needed their dad. Not because he thought Roy was any role model, but because Wade didn't want the responsibility, didn't want to put his own plans on hold. That had always been his problem—trying to get out of what other people expected of him.

Well, it was far too late to change it all now. All he could do was fulfill her last wish and care for them the best he knew how.

Wade sighed, closed the front door and strolled down the street toward the local café. When a light breeze ruffled the apple blossoms overhead and fluttered their petals to the ground, Wade thought he heard sweet, joyful laughter from the librarian's house across the back alley. He ignored it and kept walking. If he didn't get something to eat soon, his stomach was going to devour his backbone. Too bad it wouldn't be steak.

Three weeks later Clarissa picked up the basket holding a pot pie made from her grandmother's famous recipe. In the other hand she snuggled a basket of homemade biscuits and the carrier that protected her triple chocolate fudge cake—the one that had won a blue ribbon at the state fair.

"I don't care what he says," she told herself firmly as she forced open the back gate. "I promised those kids a decent meal tonight, and I am going to deliver. He can rant and rave for another two weeks if he wants. It's no skin off my nose."

But she hated the acrimony. She knew how hard it was for him to manage everything. The kids had told her enough for Clarissa to get the picture. Wade Featherhawk had not had an easy life and by the sounds of it, he wasn't scheduled for a reprieve anytime soon.

Apparently life on the reservation he'd grown up on, had not been a picnic. According to the kids, there was little work and lots of bad memories. Once he'd packed the kids up and left, he'd had to fight for every opportunity to prove he did quality work. Not that he deserved a second chance, her brain piped up. He's too cranky. But she wouldn't dream of slighting someone's work ethic just because he was in a bad humor.

Clarissa had heard the talk in town, of course. Awful bigoted talk about his heritage. There had even been rumors. Not that she paid them any heed. She encouraged those who had hired him to speak openly about Wade's good solid work ethic, and the able way he completed the jobs he contracted to do. She'd asked to keep one of the extremely good sketches he'd drawn for a renovation, and showed it to several ladies she knew wanted work done on their homes.

Gradually, people in Waseka were coming to accept the little family as a permanent fixture. Or they would do if they could only stop talking about how needy the children always looked. As a hint on her behalf, Clarissa felt it was blatantly overdone.

She'd done what she could, of course. But it wasn't easy with Wade's orders to stay away ringing in her ears. Last night Pierce's grumble had torn a sympathetic hole in her heart, and she was determined to repair it one way or another.

Clarissa stepped out her back door and peered across the lane, checking to make sure *he* wasn't around. It was too early for him, of course. And he couldn't know that she always took Wednesday afternoons off, or that his kids' sitter, Mrs. Anders, had to cancel out for this afternoon.

Feeling like a burglar, she crept across her backyard, managed to yank the gate open and carry her booty across the way without dropping a thing. Jared let her into his yard with a wide smile, his lanky height towering over her.

"Hey, something smells excellent, Clarissa."

"Why, thank you!" She felt the heat rise in her cheeks. "I hope you enjoy it." She watched him peering in the bushes. "What are you doing?"

"Trying to find my football. I have practice tonight, and I need it."

"Oh." Clarissa nodded at the basket. "If you'll carry these inside, I'll help you look."

Ten minutes later, her shoes muddy from traipsing through the garden, Clarissa found the missing ball behind the shed.

"Wow, thanks, Clarissa!" As he took the ball, Jared glanced up and frowned, his eyes on the kitchen window. "Uh-oh. Tildy's in the kitchen again."

"That's because I said I'd help her with her home ec project. Jared, do you think you could mow the grass? It's awfully long." Clarissa wasn't sure grass this long could be mowed, but it was either try to cut it now or declare the yard a part of the rain forest.

"It's bad, I know." Jared's thin cheeks went a faint pink. "I'm supposed to do it every week, but our mower is broken. Uncle Wade just hasn't had time to fix it."

"Go across the alley and get mine, then. Okay?" She waited for his nod, then went inside, confident that he knew what he was doing. After all, she'd been paying him to do her yard work for two weeks now.

Tildy stood in the kitchen, peering into the oven.

"What are you doing, honey?"

"It's not getting brown," the young girl told her. "Our home ec teacher said the crust should be golden brown."

Clarissa smiled as she closed the oven door. "The crust will get brown, just give it time. It's supposed to bake for at least an hour at a low temperature. Now, what's the project for tonight?"

"Coleslaw. I got the cabbage, but I don't know what else to do with it."

She looked so forlorn Clarissa couldn't help but smile.

"Okay, coleslaw it is. But we'll need some room. Let's do a little cleaning first." Tildy frowned, but Clarissa wasn't giving up. Opportunity didn't knock that often. "If you load the cutlery into the sink, it can soak for a few minutes while we wipe down the counter. Put the glasses in, too."

She showed the young girl how to organize everything efficiently so that a minimum amount of time was needed to clean.

"See, it doesn't take that long," she murmured, half an hour later, surveying the sparkling room with satisfaction. "Just don't let it get so far next time. Remember the first rule?"

Tildy nodded. "Clean up as you go," she repeated.

"Good. Now, where's the cabbage?"

Clarissa managed to show Tildy how to mix the dressing and got her started on slicing the cabbage into tiny strips before Lacey burst into the room, her face a mass of frustration.

"I'll never ace this dumb old biology," she muttered. "I don't even know where to get a frog."

"By the creek. There are always lots of them in the spring." Clarissa offered to help her catch one later that evening. "Hi, Pierce," she greeted as the young boy looked in through the screen door. "What's the matter?"

"There's a bird out here that I can't name. And I have to. It's important for my collection."

"Okay, well I've got a book—"

The doorbell cut across her response.

"Isn't anyone going to answer that?"

"I can't stop now. I'm just getting good at this." Tildy chewed her bottom lip as she concentrated on the thin strips of cabbage.

"Fine, I'll get it." Clarissa walked through the living room and opened the door. She almost groaned aloud. "Rita," she greeted, calmly enough. "Can I help you?"

"I doubt it. I'm here in response to the petition to adopt these children. I have to check out their home conditions." Social worker Rita Rotheby surged inside with all the pomp and ceremony of a battleship bound for duty as she tried to sidestep Clarissa. "Excuse me."

"Uh, Wade isn't here right now, Rita. Maybe it would be better if you waited until he came home." Clarissa could picture his face if he walked in right now and found *her* there.

"Nonsense! Part of the information gathering has

to be done when he's absent. To see how the children are managing."

Okay, then. It was up to her, Clarissa decided. She'd have to make sure this inspection went well.

"The children are fine. Jared is cutting the lawn."

"Unsupervised?" Rita scribbled something down.

"I'm here," Clarissa reminded her and had the satisfaction of seeing the woman erase the words. "Tildy is making coleslaw for her home ec project. Lacey is doing her biology and Pierce is cataloging birds." She trailed behind the other woman, but stopped short when Rita dragged a finger over the kitchen counter. Surely she hadn't missed a spot?

"You have dinner already made?" the woman asked Tildy in disbelief.

"Yes, and she's got all the major food groups covered, too. Isn't it great?" Clarissa smiled at Tildy, willing her to smile back. "As you can see, Rita, Wade is doing a fine job with these children."

"Hm. Things do seem to have changed. For the better." Rita inspected the laundry room and found the machines purring.

Clarissa breathed a thank you that she'd thought to start a couple of loads earlier. She followed Rita back through the house. With all the finesse of a person who has a right to be in someone else's home, she opened the front door and smiled her best hostess smile. "Everything's fine, Rita."

"Well, it does seem to be. I'll file this and send a copy of it to Mr. Featherhawk. I don't like to do anything behind anyone's back." Rita surged through the door, then stopped. "Oh, there you are. I must tell you, sir, that I found a vast improvement this time. Keep up the good work." Having given her blessing, Rita bustled down the sidewalk to her car.

Clarissa gulped, gaping at the frowning face of Wade Featherhawk. He glanced at Rita's disappearing back, then at Clarissa, then at the house.

"It's nice someone in this town is honest about their intentions." His voice chewed her out for her insolence. "I thought I asked you to leave us alone."

Clarissa carefully shut the door behind him, checked to make sure no children were around, then faced him.

"Yes, you did. And I tried to respect your wishes. But I was asked over here to help out. And I was glad to do it." She held her head up, daring him to question her further. "Now that you're here, I'll be on my way." She turned her back and walked toward the kitchen.

"There's a load of jeans in the washer and a bunch of your shirts in the dryer. You might want to take those out before they wrinkle. Tildy, you've done very well with that cabbage, although I think you've cut a bit more than you need. Just follow the recipe I left there and you'll be fine. Bye for now." And gathering up her purse, Clarissa headed for the back door.

She'd hoped to get away without another lecture, but it was obvious that Wade wasn't prepared to let this go.

"I'll walk you out." His fingers wrapped around her elbow determinedly.

Clarissa marched out the back door, down the

steps and across the newly mown yard. Jared was now working at the side of the house.

"He must have fixed it," Wade muttered, staring at the shorn lawn. He shook his head and focused on her. "I don't know how many times I have to say this, Miss Cartwright."

"Don't bother! I already know what you're going to say. You've told me enough times."

She kept on walking. Or she would have if he'd let go of her arm.

"Then why—"

"Why do I keep coming back here?" She rounded on him angrily. "Because *they* asked me to, that's why. And I can't say no." She gulped down her frustration. "I know you don't want me here, but the children need my help. And so do you."

"No, I don't." He enunciated each word with frustrated precision.

"Well, you need something. Rita is the head honcho around here, and Judge Prendergast will do whatever she recommends. If you don't get her on your side, you're going to lose those kids to the state welfare agency. Is that what you want?"

"No, of course not!" Wade raked a hand through his hair, his face weary. "But I can't be here all the time. I can't do everything."

"I know," Clarissa told him calmly. "That's why it makes sense for them to come to me. I'd love to help and I don't mind in the least. I like them. I think they're smart kids."

"But I don't want them to become dependent on you. They shouldn't have to lose someone again. That's not fair to them."

Clarissa shrugged. "Is it fair that you lock a *friend* out of their lives, won't even let me help a little by providing a meal now and again? Is it fair that Lacey and Pierce and Jared and Tildy all come to me for help and I have to send them away because you're too stubborn to accept a little assistance once in a while?" She said the words that had begged release for days now.

"Is it fair that I can't mother them a little?"

"Probably not," he agreed grimly. "I don't think it's fair that their mother died, either. Or that I—" He stopped, clenched his jaw, then shrugged. "It's just the way life has to be."

Clarissa saw red. The hidden words poured out of her mouth with no regard for the consternation spreading across his glowering face.

"No, it doesn't! Can't you see that I only want to help these kids? I'm not asking you to be involved," she added scornfully. "And I'm not after your money or your house or anything like that."

"No, you're after my kids." His eyes glinted belligerently.

"All right! Yes, I am. I'm asking you to consider them and what it must be like to grow up like this. They can't have friends over because there's no one here to supervise."

"I hired someone." His chin jutted out as if to say "so there."

"I know." Clarissa nodded. "Mrs. Anders. She couldn't come this afternoon so she asked me to stop in once they were home from school. But it's not the same." She continued. "They haven't any spare time to go out with chums because there are so many chores.'' She waved a hand at the house behind them.

"You talk about my house being run-down, but at least it has more than one bathroom and lots of bedrooms. This place is too small!''

As she searched his face for a hint of acquiescence, Clarissa let her heart's desire pour out. ''Why would it be so wrong to let me coddle them a little bit? I promise I'm not after you. I know I'm not wife material—I'm not beautiful or desirable or any of those things men want in a wife, but that doesn't matter, does it? I can still be a friend to them, and a darn good one! I can love these kids and be there for them. Why won't you let me? They'll still love you, Wade. I would never do anything to change that.''

Wade stared at her, his mouth hanging open. He reached out and lifted a strand of her hair and tucked it back behind her ear, his fingers brushing against her cheek. When he finally spoke, his voice was quiet, sober. Clarissa steeled herself for the rebuff she knew would come.

"There's nothing wrong with your looks, Miss Cartwright. You have a soft-spoken kind of beauty that any man in his right mind would find attractive. But I'm not that man. I have nothing to give. It's all I can do to provide for four children. I don't need a wife to look after, too.''

"Actually, I was in no way suggesting that. But those children are exactly why you do need a wife,'' she countered, then stopped as the grim line returned to his mouth. ''I'm not proposing, Wade. Really, I'm not! But will you at least let me help out once in a while? Will you come over for a meal now and then?

Will you let me help Pierce with his birds and Lacey with her biology? Just until you've got things more settled?''

Wade studied her for a long time, but when he spoke there was a hint of amusement in his low tones. "Frankly, I'd be ecstatic if you'd take over Lacey's biology. It's a subject I detest, especially the dissecting. And you know very well that Pierce has never stopped questioning you about his collection, in spite of my protests.''

It was an admission, but Clarissa wanted more.

"And you'll come for dinner? Tomorrow? No, Friday. You'll let me help Tildy with her school cooking stuff?'' She waited, her breath held till it hurt her chest.

"We'll come for dinner on Saturday,'' he finally agreed. "And I suppose it won't hurt for Tildy to get some help, once in a while. But that's all. Nothing more. You won't drop over and clean the house or mend clothes or do the laundry.'' His eyes narrowed suspiciously. "Do you promise you won't pretend there's something more going on when the busybodies start talking?''

"Of course not!'' Clarissa was scandalized by the very idea. "I'm just a friend, and I'd like to help you out.''

"Fine. Then I'll help out, too.'' He sniffed. "Whatever's cooking in that oven didn't come from Tildy's hands. In repayment for your assistance, I'll fix your roof.''

"Oh, but it's just a chicken pie!'' She frowned, trying to imagine how much fixing her roof would cost him. "I didn't expect you to—''

"Take it or leave it," he warned, but there was a glint in his eye that warmed her heart. "If you help us, we help you. Friends."

Her decision was unfairly influenced by the drop of rain on her nose. "I'll take it. I've got to get going."

"To put pails out, no doubt. You should have had it fixed months ago." Wade shook his head as he surveyed the sorry condition of her weathered gables and red-rimmed turrets. "I'll come over tomorrow and take a look."

"You don't have to—"

His look silenced her.

"All right. Thank you very much. I'll be at the library till eight. We stay open late on Thursday."

"I know. Believe me, I think I've been told everything about you." He didn't make it sound like a compliment.

"Really?" Clarissa frowned. "Like what?"

"You have this," one finger trailed across her jaw where it curved up to meet her ear, touching the hairline scar, "because, at age six, you helped get Johnny McCabe out of a tumble-down barn. You broke this arm when Petey Somebody dared you to jump off a granary, and Sarah Kingsley stopped being your best friend when she stole all your doll babies in grade two."

Clarissa gaped at him, nodding her head as he spoke.

"Mercy, they must be serious," she whispered. "The townsfolk haven't told anyone that stuff since Harrison."

He frowned. "Harrison? Harrison was the man

you were engaged to. He dumped you when your old friend came back to town. He married her instead of you.'' Wade's voice held a hint of sympathy. ''What a jerk!''

''Harrison wasn't a jerk,'' she murmured, staring into Wade's knowing gaze. ''He was just confused. I wasn't what he wanted, but Grace was. She was very beautiful, just like a model. I couldn't compete with that.''

''He was a fool. Beauty goes a lot deeper than the skin.'' Wade's hand dropped away from her face as he took a deep breath. His eyes hardened. ''But don't get any ideas, Miss Cartwright. I'm not in the market for a wife. And I am *not* Harrison's replacement. Not in a million years.''

The pain he inflicted with those words bit deep and it was all she could do not to burst into tears. She didn't want someone to replace Harrison! She wanted someone better than him, a man who would think she was as wonderful as Harrison found Grace; she wanted a storybook kind of love.

Clarissa walked out of his yard, crossed the alley and yanked her own gate open. She stopped, turned and stared at him, only then realizing that he'd followed her.

''No, you're not him,'' she agreed quietly. ''I don't think anyone could ever replace Harrison in my life.'' Then she closed the gate, walked across the yard and into her big empty house.

''Harrison was a sign,'' she whispered as she stared out the window at the falling rain. ''A sign that I'm supposed to be alone. And you, Wade Featherhawk, just confirmed it.''

She forgot all about the pails as tears, hot and bitter, coursed down her cheeks. How it hurt, to have those children there and not to be able to love them as she wanted, to mother them.

"It doesn't matter," she sobbed to the Lord, determination setting her jaw. "I'll be their mother in my heart. He can't stop me from loving them. No one can."

But as the tears dried and her heart calmed, Clarissa couldn't help remembering the look on Wade's face. He'd *wanted* to let her help, wanted to let her in. She'd seen that.

So why didn't he? Why was he so afraid to trust, let her into his world?

Chapter Three

Eight weeks to the day after he'd moved to Waseka, Wade pulled up to the curb in front of his house at five minutes to six, and parked, grinding the gears as he hadn't done since he was thirteen. He forced himself to open the truck door, even though every muscle in his body begged him to just sit there and vegetate.

Man, he was tired. He couldn't ever remember being this bone weary before. His eyes were bleary and unfocused and his hand wasn't steady. Maybe if he put his head down, just for a moment, maybe then he could get his second wind. Or third.

"Wade?"

Oh, no, not *her* again! Wade huffed out a great puff of air, his brain groaning. What now?

"Wade, I think you'd better open your eyes and listen to me."

Clarissa's soft voice sounded deadly serious. He blinked his eyes open. Her face was white. Of course, it was always pale, but now it had lost all color. Her eyes were red and her hands blackened, as if she'd been playing in the dirt. There were the smudges all over her long floaty skirt.

How many times had he dreamed of that skirt?

"Wade? There was a fire."

He jerked awake, his brain revving into high gear. "The kids?"

"They're fine. They're at my place." She took a deep breath. "That's not all."

Not all? Wasn't that enough? What else could there be? He tried to focus on what she was saying. "Huh?"

"Rita was here today, doing another inspection. She's, um, pretty steamed."

"Why?" He eased himself out of the truck, knowing he had to move but wincing at every budge of his smarting muscles. "What happened?"

"You'd better look for yourself."

Her delicate hands helped him stumble to the sidewalk and up the path. She pushed open the front door and guided him inside.

The living room was littered with stuff, as usual. Smoky, water-soaked stuff, he noticed. Dishes cluttered the kitchen counter and food sat on the table as flies buzzed over it. A huge black spot covered the ceiling, most of the stove and a section of the floor.

He shuddered, immediately alert to the fact that he could hear no children's voices. "What happened?"

"Tildy was frying. The oil caught on fire."

That woke him up. He gulped at the idea of his lovely young niece covered in burns.

"She was trying to help Pierce and forgot to pay

attention. Jared saw it start and thought he could put it out with a dish towel. That caught on fire too." She pointed to the corner. "The oil set the cloth alight and when he tossed it to the floor, it caught onto the laundry Lacey was going to wash. I saw smoke and came over. By the time I got here, Pierce had finally found a fire extinguisher and put it out, but by then Rita had already arrived."

"But where was Mrs. Anders?"

"Apparently the hospital called to say her husband had a heart attack. She told the kids to call me when she couldn't reach you, but they didn't want to be a bother. I think Tildy was afraid I'd make her wait to fry. She's desperate to get an A in that class."

It was clear to Wade by the glint in her eyes that Clarissa felt the children were reciting his precise words. He clenched his fists, drew a breath and summoned all his courage.

"And? You might as well spit out the rest of it." His heart dropped to his boots as he surveyed the damage and considered how much worse off they could have been.

"Rita told me to take the kids. I wanted to call you but no one knew where you were." There was a hint of censure in her voice. "I tried to stall her, but she'd already made her decision by then."

Wade saw her swallow, heard her voice drop, and knew the worst had happened.

"I think she's going to recommend foster care, Wade."

"She can't!" He couldn't bear the thought of it, his sister's kids split apart, separated, living with people who wouldn't understand them. His own life, empty and barren of the joy they brought, the small glimpses of his sister he caught in each child. Worst of all, the promise would be broken.

He shook his head, refusing to accept it. "She can't."

"Yes, Wade. She can. I just wanted to warn you." Clarissa didn't meet his glance, but stood staring at her feet, her head bowed in sadness.

Wade stared at the mess he'd made of things. "I should have been here, should have been nearby. Why did I have to pick this afternoon to run to the city for supplies?"

"It doesn't matter now." Her head lifted as if she'd come to some decision. She studied his face for a long moment, then tugged at his arm. "Come on, Wade."

"It does matter." He felt the responsibility and almost bowed under it. "It's my fault. It's *all* my fault. They could have died. I should have managed better. No matter how hard I try, I never seem to get it right. I messed up here. Again." He couldn't look her in the eye, knew he'd see condemnation.

Clarissa's fingers tightened on his arm. "I'm sure you've done the best you could. No one was hurt. And it's not anyone's fault. Accidents happen." She pushed against his chest. "Come with me. I've already called the insurance agency. It's the only one in town, remember. Your renter's policy covers most of the damage, they think. But you can't stay here. Not till they've assessed the damage."

He stared at her, his mind numb with the realization that his little family was now homeless. His brain wouldn't move on from that. He felt the tug on his arm as if through a fog. "Oh. No, I suppose not. Thank you."

"You're welcome. Can you get up?"

Dimly Wade realized that sometime during their conversation he'd flopped down onto one of the kitchen chairs. His eyes noted the places where fire had singed the flooring, and he shivered at the thought of what might have happened.

"Wade?"

"What?" He blinked and refocused on her, forcing his mind to function. "Oh. Get up? Why?"

"You need a shower and something to eat, for one thing. You can have that at my place. The water heater's turned off here. The firemen said it was better that way. Come on."

He managed to get up and stumble to the back door, grateful for her calm even voice and the gentle hand under his arm. His brain couldn't take it all in. It was like a bad dream.

A pile of charred bits of fabric lay outside the back door. Wade stopped in his tracks and stared. He couldn't seem to move his eyes away, couldn't stop imagining the scars...

"Wade, listen to me." Clarissa turned his face toward her, her palms cool again his cheeks.

She felt good, he decided. Soothing. He didn't even try to free himself. Her flower-soft fragrance tickled his nose. Roses, he thought. Or lavender maybe. Something like his mother would have worn.

Her eyes were clear and calm. "You have to get out of here now, Wade. Everybody is fine. They're okay. Come on, let's keep going."

He moved on only because he knew she would

nag him until he did. He walked across the grass, and into her yard with its pretty flowers and trim grass, marveling at the contrast between the two houses. His fingers curled around her small soft hand. Such a tiny hand to be so competent.

"I'm fine," he mumbled when her other hand slid under his arm. He forced his rubber legs to move one foot in front of the other.

"Of course you are. Three steps up now." There was a hint of amused mockery in her quiet tones.

"I'm just worried about the kids. My boots—"

"Are fine." She urged him inside. "Sit down here and drink this."

He took the cup from her fingers and sipped the dark steaming brew. "I don't take sugar."

"Today you do. Drink it." There was no room for argument in that prim order.

Wade drank, his mind picturing that awful scene again.

"They're fine, Wade. See, there's Pierce working on his birds in the front yard. And Tildy's sitting out there, too. With Ryan Adams. Lacey's over in the park. You can just see her red shirt through the trees." She pointed.

Wade followed the direction and caught sight of Lacey's favorite blouse. "Jared?" he choked, his heart swelling with relief.

"I'm right here. I'm trying to fix this stupid—uh, broken cupboard." Jared came to stand before his uncle. He frowned. "You don't look too good, Uncle Wade."

"That's funny. I feel fine. Just fine." Wade noticed his sister's distinct features in the tall boy and felt the guilt wash over him again. He was growing up so fast. "Are you all right, son?"

"Of course. We all are. Clarissa's taking care of things. That's okay, isn't it, Uncle Wade?" Jared's face contorted with worry. "You're not mad that we got her? Tildy didn't mean to do it, you know. It was an accident."

"I know. No. It's perfect. Okay, I mean." Wade glanced around with bleary eyes, noting the sparkling kitchen, the yeasty fragrance of fresh baked bread, the utter hominess of it all. No matter what he did, his kitchen had never looked like this. He noticed Jared's frown and refocused.

"It's just fine," he repeated, then stopped when his stomach began a low but very audible rumbling.

"Jared, will you show your uncle where the shower is? And here are some fresh towels. As soon as he's ready, we'll have dinner." Clarissa smiled, her eyes meeting Wade's. "Go ahead. Everything is all right. I'll watch them for you. We'll talk later."

Wade followed Jared up the stairs, easing up on the balustrade when he felt it give under his weight.

"Another thing to be fixed," he muttered, trying to smother a yawn. "This house sure needs a lot of catch-up work."

"You should have let me help you finish Mac-Gregor's roof last night," Jared told him, frowning. "I can do stuff. Besides, you can't work morning, noon and night, Uncle Wade. Nobody can. You'll burn out. I heard the teachers talking about it."

"I'll do whatever it takes to make a home for you kids. I promised your mom, and I'm not breaking that promise." Wade let himself be led into the bathroom. He accepted the armload of towels and listened as Jared explained the old-fashioned shower.

"Make sure you keep that curtain in the tub or Clarissa's place will be flooded," the boy ordered, frowning up at him as if he wasn't sure Wade understood.

"Uh-huh. Curtain inside. Got it." Wade repeated the words mindlessly, unable to hang onto any thought other than that the kids were all right.

After a long searching look at his uncle, Jared left the bathroom, apparently satisfied that Wade could manage on his own. Wade grinned at such consideration, but decided it was rather endearing coming from the boy.

He stripped off his clothes, fully conscious of how much dust he was leaving in the pretty lavender-and-white bathroom. He'd spent the sunrise hours of this morning replacing hundred-year-old attic shavings with insulation so that the owners could move in right away. Most of the dust had settled somewhere on him.

As he felt the warm sting of the water trickle over his aching body, Wade closed his eyes and searched for an answer.

Please God, what should I do now? I can't give up Kendra's kids. I just can't. I promised her.

Sometime later, Wade didn't know how long, the water grew cool, then the chill of it finally penetrated to his brain. He turned the taps off and grabbed a towel, rubbing himself fiercely to warm up.

Someone, Jared maybe, had set some clean clothes on the toilet seat. He pulled them on automatically, barely noting the newly replaced buttons and carefully stitched tears.

Then he sat down to think.

He had to do something. Figure out something. He wasn't going to lose Kendra's kids. Not now. He'd promised and, no matter what it cost, this time he was keeping his promise. He wasn't going to mess up again, social worker or no.

His eye caught sight of the silk lavender bathrobe hanging on the back of the door. Clarissa was a lavender kind of woman. Her pale skin and silver-streaked hair would look perfect in the color. A pair of slippers lay on the floor, and he imagined her padding around this old house in the morning.

He'd seen her several times when he'd risen early. She always put out birdseed first thing. Then he'd catch the hint of fresh brewed coffee and pretty soon she'd be sitting at the table by the bay window, sipping it as she watched the birds peck at their meal. It took her a long time to wake up, but eventually she'd move, and Wade would catch the aroma of frying bacon or grilling sausages.

Now that the weather was warmer, she'd begun eating outside, sharing her breakfast with whatever came along. Then she'd pull up a few weeds, water her garden, finish her coffee and undo her hair.

Wade always liked watching her brush out her hair, though he felt a bit embarrassed, like a Peeping Tom or something. But once she undid that knot on top, he couldn't tear his eyes away. He would never have believed her hair was so long, not when she wound it up on the top of her head like that. Free and cascading down her back, it flowed well past her waist in a river of sparkling silver.

A shrill childish laugh penetrated his musing and Wade got up to look out the small bathroom window. Pierce was pointing at a tree and ordering everyone to look. Seconds later Clarissa came outside, a big book in her hands. She and Pierce sat together on the grass and searched through the pages until they found what they wanted. Wade watched as Pierce leaned his head on Clarissa's shoulder, his voice barely audible on the late afternoon air.

"Am I a nerd, Clarissa?"

"Of course not! I don't know many children who could identify as many birds as you can, Pierce. Why would you think such a thing?" She sounded truly amazed by his question.

"That's what the kids call me. They say it's stupid to spend so much time on birds." Pierce shrugged. "Maybe they're right. I don't play their games very well."

As Wade watched, Clarissa hugged the little boy closer.

"Listen, sweetheart. Everybody has different interests. You like birds, and there's not one thing wrong with that. There's nothing wrong with games, either. The problem comes when we make fun of other people for their choices."

"But I don't fit in! I don't even know how to catch a ball."

Pierce's rueful tones told Wade that catching a ball was very important, and Wade chewed himself out for not spending more time with the boy.

"Then we'll have to practice. That's not such a

hard thing to learn. Not like a baby bird learning to fly, for goodness sake." Clarissa's beautiful smile coaxed him to join in and a minute later Pierce called his big brother to help him practice.

"She's good," Wade muttered to himself in admiration. "She's very, very good with them."

"I got the frog, but I lost the guy." That was Lacey, glum with disappointment as she flopped down on the lawn beside Clarissa. "What is it with this biology stuff?"

"Oh? Didn't Kevin want to study with you?" Clarissa sounded amused. "He certainly rushed over here quickly when he heard about the fire."

Wade frowned. Who the dickens was Kevin? And what did the kid want with *his* niece?

"Kevin had to go home for supper." Lacey sprawled on the grass, bare feet nestling into Clarissa's skirt. "Honestly, he's so smart, I feel like a dud."

"He's not smart about everything." Clarissa fiddled with her skirt, but Wade caught the glimmer of a smile twitching at the corners of her mouth. "I happen to know that he's only recently taken to studying biology. You might ask him for help with your own work."

"You mean like spend a date dissecting a frog?" Lacey made a face. "Ugh!"

"Well, why not? You'd get to spend time together. Anyway, you're too young to date."

Wade watched as Clarissa rose lithely to her feet, her hand gently smoothing the other girl's hair.

"Think about it," she murmured. "I've got to

check the kitchen. I think Tildy's forgotten something."

Wade adjusted his position and spotted the tiny funnel cloud of smoke coming out the back screen door. He groaned. "How many times is it going to take for that girl?"

When no one answered him, he realized he was talking to himself. Gathering up his dirty clothes, he headed downstairs to face the reality of his messed-up life.

"Tildy, honey, you have to set the timer. Then things won't burn, even if you do forget. The timer will remind you."

"How many cakes is that?" Tildy's tearful voice warned Wade that she'd been at it for a while. So did the acrid odor of smoldering sugar.

"It's only a bit of flour and sugar, Tildy. It doesn't matter. We'll just try again after supper. Okay?"

A huge sigh. "Okay. Thanks a lot, Clarissa. I really appreciate it."

"You're welcome, sweetie."

Wade walked in just as Clarissa hugged his niece. He stood there, studying their obvious camaraderie for a long time. It was only when she touched his arm, that he realized Clarissa had been speaking to him. He jerked to attention, pushing his thoughts away. "Sorry. What did you say?"

"I'll take the clothes and put them in the washer. You sit down. We're all ready." In a matter of seconds she had the others gathered around her worn oak table. "I'll just say grace."

Wade automatically bowed his head, listening to her few soft words of thanks.

"Now, if you could slice this roast, we'll be all ready." She handed him the carving knife and a platter with a piece of succulent beef sitting in the middle of it, juices dark and tantalizingly pooled around it.

Wade watched as she set out a heaping dish of mashed potatoes, peas, gravy, fresh rolls and a salad. His mouth watered. His stomach rumbled again, more loudly this time. The kids burst out laughing.

And suddenly, with piercing clarity, he knew exactly what he had to do. Wade set down the carving knife beside his plate, focusing his entire attention on Clarissa's face.

"I need to say something before we start."

"Yes?" Clarissa looked up from pouring Pierce a glass of milk. There was mild interest in her eyes, but nothing more. It was obvious that she had no idea of his intentions.

"Clarissa, uh…" He stopped, looked around and realized that everyone was staring at him. He couldn't do this now, not here, in front of the kids!

"Yes?" Clarissa set the milk jug down on the counter, seated herself and carefully spread her napkin in her lap. "Pass the potatoes around, please, Jared."

Wade frowned. He really should do this properly, in private, where she'd pay full attention to him, listen to all his arguments. Yeah, later.

He glanced around the table. The kids were gawking at him, their mouths hanging open in amazement as he ladled yet another spoonful of peas onto his plate.

"I didn't know you liked peas so much, Uncle

Wade.'' Tildy almost hid the laugh that tilted up the side of her pretty mouth.

''What? Oh. Sorry. Here, Pierce, take some of these.'' He pushed half the plateful onto the boy's plate, opened one of the golden rolls and watched the butter he spread on it melt into a puddle of soft creamy yellow.

Yes, marriage was the only way to go now. He didn't have a choice, not if he intended to keep his promise. His wants, needs, had to come second to what was best for the kids. With Clarissa as their stepmother, no court could deny the children her tender caring. He could only hope she still wanted a family.

''Clarissa, I—'' He stopped again, searching for the right way to ask her for a date. Sort of. Not a real date, of course.

''Go ahead, Wade. I'm listening.'' She smiled that gentle, Mona-Lisa-like smile that made his palms sweat, but her attention wasn't on him. ''Use your fork please, Pierce. Tildy, would you open the window a bit more? It's quite hot in here. What did you want to say, Wade?''

When no answer was forthcoming after several minutes, Clarissa looked up. She stopped spooning out potatoes for just one moment, stared at him inquisitively, then glanced around the table at the curious faces that watched him so closely. Finally, she broke the silence, her eyes darker as they studied him.

''Go ahead, children. Eat your dinner. We've some homework to do later. Your uncle is tired. Let him relax.''

Everyone else seemed to follow her lead as one by one, the kids took up the signal, dishing up her food like locusts on a field of tender green shoots. Soon the conversation was going a mile a minute. Wade decided to go with the flow. He picked up the salad and filled his bowl.

"Clarissa's house is a great place, Uncle Wade. Do you know she's got a screen porch back there? I'm gonna sit out there tonight and watch the fireflies. Some people around here call them lightning bugs. Isn't that a silly name?"

Pierce chatted away a mile a minute, and Wade let him, content to eat while he examined Clarissa's ability to get his whole family involved in the conversation.

How did she do that? The most he got some nights was a grunt or a heap of complaints. Of course, it wasn't while they were eating food like this!

Jared looked pleased by his reasoning.

"Yeah! And we can live in this house, right, Uncle Wade? For a little while anyway." He grinned happily. "I love this old house. It's kinda like staying with an old friend. It's got some problems, but it's homey."

The words stabbed Wade with the wealth of longing he could hear beneath those words. He had no idea the boy felt that way. When had they ever hung around anywhere long enough to make old friends? Of course, he'd lost a lot. Kendra had a knack for making her house a home, probably because she'd loved her kids so much.

"I think it's a romantic house with all these crocheted curtains, and especially those frilly things over Clarissa's bed.''

Lacey sighed and hugged herself in a melodramatic way that Wade knew meant she'd been reading sappy love stories again. Oh well, she'd run into reality soon enough. Why spoil the illusion of happy ever after?

"If we lived here all the time, I could take all kinds of pictures of the birds. Clarissa's got way better birds than we have, plus she's got the woods right out there. We've just got that dumb old playground, and the noise scares them away. Can I have some more meat? Please?''

The topic of the conversation said nothing, merely smiling at the children as they talked and munching on the minuscule amounts of food she placed on her own plate.

Though Wade spent a long time studying her, Clarissa did not return his look. She waited, hands folded in her lap, until everyone was finished, then gathered up the plates.

"Would anyone like some peach cobbler?'' She lifted a golden delicacy from the oven. "I have some ice cream to go with it.''

Wade closed his eyes and breathed. Heaven help him! Peach cobbler was his favorite dessert. And no one had ever made it better than his sister. The words brought back fond memories of their times together on the reservation when they'd had to depend on each other for companionship. They'd picked peaches one year and earned enough money to buy bikes. They'd also taken home cases and cases of the ripened peaches, until his mother had begged them to stop.

How had Clarissa found out?

Wade jerked up his head to study her, his eyes narrowed as he tried to search out some hint that she'd known about his past. But Clarissa simply stared at him with that bland smile, holding out a dish, ice cream melting on top, as she waited patiently for his response.

"Oh, I'm sorry," she murmured when he didn't take it. "Perhaps you'd rather have something else? I know some people don't care for peaches."

"I'll try it," Wade managed to say and took the dish from her hand. "Thank you."

"You're quite welcome. Coffee?"

Wade *tried* three helpings of the dessert, and by then he knew that he'd done the right thing in deciding to propose to her. A man didn't find a woman like Clarissa Cartwright every day, not one who made peach cobbler that melted in your mouth, or one who could dissect a frog without wincing. There sure weren't many women who'd calmly take in five people, feed, shelter and care for them as if it weren't a stitch out of the usual routine.

He'd better hang on to her before somebody else beat him to the punch. After all, hadn't she been praying to get married the day he'd met her? Wade was pretty sure he wasn't an answer to prayer, but she would get her family. That ought to make a difference.

"We'll do the dishes, Clarissa. You and Uncle Wade go have coffee on the veranda," Tildy ordered. "I'm sure you have things to talk about."

Wade noticed a sparkle in her eye that hadn't been there before. Had his niece figured out what he was going to do? If she had, Wade dearly hoped she'd shut up about it until he got everything arranged.

Would Clarissa agree to his preposterous scheme?

He helped the thin, silent woman into the big woven willow chair, handed her a cup of well-creamed coffee, then took his own seat. He set down his mug and faced her.

"Clarissa?"

"Yes?" She calmly sipped her drink, her eyes on the blooming apple tree in the garden outside.

Wade felt his temperature begin to rise at her obvious disinterest in what he was saying. For the kids, he reminded himself as he licked a crumb of peach cobbler off the edge of his lip. He was doing this for the kids.

"Would you marry me?"

"Oh, I don't think so." She said it so matter-of-factly, he wasn't sure he'd heard right.

"What? Why not?" he demanded.

"Because you only want someone to look after the kids until you can get things straight with Rita. We can do that without getting married." She avoided his eyes, peering up into the sky instead. "You don't have to marry me to get my help. I've already offered a number of times. Remember?"

Wade flushed. He'd been rude with his refusal, and he'd hurt her feelings. Besides, what woman wanted to be proposed to like that? He could at least make this part of it special. He opened his mouth and then clamped it shut as she spoke.

"Don't worry about it, Wade. It will all work out.

Everything will be fine. You'll see. You just have to trust God to handle these things.''

He took a deep breath, hating the idea of spilling his guts, but knowing he was going to have to open up a little, let her inside. He hated that, hated feeling exposed and vulnerable to anyone. It only made it easier to see how many mistakes he'd made.

So why did he have this strange feeling that he could count on *this* woman?

"I do trust God, but I am also worried, Clarissa. I made a pact with my sister. Before she died, I promised I would take care of her kids, that I'd keep them together, raise them as my own. I vowed that I wouldn't let them get into the trouble I've had.'' He gulped. "So far, I'm doing a lousy job.''

"I think you're doing very well.'' Clarissa motioned toward his house. "That was just an accident. I'm sure Rita will come to understand that. In time.''

"It's an accident that shouldn't have happened. I should have done better for them. They need someone to help them through the tough parts. I wasn't thinking properly, you see. I thought giving them a home and food and a sense of security was what they needed most.''

Clarissa smiled, her face thoughtful. "It's a good deal to ask of anyone,'' she murmured. "The children have done very well under your care.''

He flushed with pleasure. "Maybe. But I have a hunch they'd do even better with you as their stepmother.'' He said it deliberately, wanting to shake her out of this Mona Lisa stupor she'd sunken into. When that didn't work, Wade kept talking.

"I'm not very good at listening to what they're

not saying, to finding out what's bothering them. And I can't be there all the time, even though I'd like to be. But I really do want the best for them.''

Clarissa nodded. "You don't have to convince me. I know that anybody who got to love those children would be very happy.'' She said it mildly, her fingers busy fiddling with her skirt again. It was the only sign that she was in the least bit nervous, but Wade took courage from that.

"So, will you marry me?"

She shook her head. "No. I don't think so."

Wade huffed out a sigh, half anger, half frustration. "I don't get it. You love kids, you want to be married, you're not involved with anyone else. Are you?'' He frowned, then relaxed when she shook her head.

"No."

"So why not? I'm not an ogre. I do an honest job. I'm fair with my employers and with the kids. I'm certainly not rich, but we're managing. What else is there?''

"Love."

The whispered word made him frown. "Clarissa, I've told you I like you. I think you're a very special person.'' He couldn't say more than that, couldn't tell her that he thought she had grit and gumption and an inner strength that he admired. It wasn't, well, romantic.

Clarissa shook her head as she smiled, her eyes avoiding his. "I'm not talking about special. *Special* is a mean-anything word.'' It was clear that she held little stock in the term. "I'm talking about love, Wade. The real thing that holds marriages together long after the children have left and the attraction has gone. The deep abiding commitment that two people make to each other until death does them part.''

''But that's what I'm offering. At least...'' Wade was beginning to wish he'd never opened his big mouth. A man shouldn't have to work this hard to convince someone to marry him!

''Uh-uh.'' She shook her head again and a few curling tendrils tumbled loose of her topknot. ''You see me as this sad spinster woman who's shriveling up inside, don't you? And maybe I am. But I believe in the power of love to change people, to change lives.'' She finally met his stare, her eyes intent. ''Do you?''

He nodded slowly, visualizing the kids in ten years. ''I believe your love could transform those children into even better adults. And you do love them, don't you, Clarissa?'' He waited, hoping she wouldn't deny what was so obviously the truth.

''Of course.'' She didn't even bother to pretend.

''So do I. And that's what this is all about. You and I are adults. We know the score, we know how many marriages fail even *with* love. We also know that lots of people have happy marriages without love.'' He took a deep breath and continued, praying for guidance through this minefield.

''I'm offering a commitment to you. I won't walk out on you or them, Clarissa. I will never walk away. I like you. I respect and admire you. And I want you to marry me.''

''For the children?''

He nodded. ''I won't lie. For the children. To keep

them together, to give them the kind of home they won't have if they go into foster care. Because I think you care enough about them to help me keep them together.''

She sat back in her chair, her eyes closed, head tilted back against the soft cushion as if she were praying. Wade sat there, studying her. Even with only her grandmother, Wade knew she'd enjoyed all the things he'd missed out on in his childhood, all the things he wanted for the kids.

''It would be good for you, too. You want a family, somebody to eat all that wonderful cooking, to share this place. Someone to laugh with and enjoy life. I know you'd be taking on an awful lot, but I believe you're the kind of woman who can do that and enjoy it.'' Hadn't he seen that for himself? Wade let a tiny bit of his heart unfold to her.

''This way, you'd get to mother the kids the way you would your own. You wouldn't have to work if you didn't want to. I'd provide a home for us, either here or in a new place altogether, if that's what you want.''

She was watching him now, her eyes shadowed, hiding her thoughts. Wade couldn't tell if she was buying into the dream or not, so he played the only card he had left.

''Love could happen, Clarissa. Maybe someday. You're a very beautiful woman, you know. When you relax and forget to be so prim and prissy, your natural beauty shines through. That's why the kids latched on to you so quick. They're good judges of character.''

If Wade was sure of one thing in his life it was

that Clarissa Cartwright was decent, caring, loyal and true. She wouldn't run away or back out of a deal because of something in his past. So there was no need to tell her.

Was there?

Her huffy voice broke into his thoughts. "I am not in the least prim!"

"Yes, you are. But in the nicest way." He grinned. He was getting to her, he could tell.

Silence.

Then she spoke again.

"All right, Wade." Her voice carried to him softly, barely audible above the crickets. "I will marry you. For the children."

A wave of relief swelled, then cascaded all over him. Wade sighed his relief, stood and drew her up to stand beside him. In the dim light from the living room he could barely see into her eyes. She looked soft, vulnerable in the wash of twilight that made her round, solemn eyes seem lonely. He wanted to reassure her that she wasn't making the biggest mistake in her life taking him on.

"No, that isn't quite right." He shook his head, suddenly wanting their relationship to be more than that. "Not just for the children. For us, too. We'll make something good of this marriage, Clarissa. I promise you that."

As he tilted her chin and leaned down to touch her lips with his in a promise, Wade shoved thoughts of the past out of his mind and concentrated on the shy, timid, butterfly-woman in his arms. Her lips were soft, untried, and he touched them reverently, asking a question.

When her arms lifted to encircle his neck and her mouth molded to his, he thought he had his answer. The tiny fire of hope flickering inside his heart told him they would make this work.

Only later, when he was checking into the motel, did it dawn on him that he was doing the one thing he'd promised himself he would never do. Wade would be starting his married life with a lie. He would never allow love to blossom in his heart.

But for now, there wasn't any other way. He needed Clarissa.

Chapter Four

"Oh, I'm so glad you're here, Blair. And you, too, Briony. You've made it the perfect day." Two weeks later Clarissa hugged her dearest friends in turn, paying careful attention not to crush her wedding dress. "It's been so long since we were all together. The three musketeers—Blair Delayney, Briony Green and Clarissa Cartwright. I miss college sometimes. We could just flop on each other's bed and chat nonstop."

"Of course we're here! We wouldn't miss this for anything! If you remember, *this*—" Blair waved a hand around the bride's room at the church "—is what we chatted about." She dabbed at her tears. "You've waited a long time, honey, and Wade is a wonderful man. I know you'll both be very happy."

"You will be happy, Prissy. I can feel it right here." Briony tapped her chest, giggling as Clarissa rolled her eyes at her indignation of that old nickname. "I only get that feeling at special times and this is one of them."

"I think you get that feeling when you eat as much pepperoni as you did last night. Try some antacids." Blair winked at Clarissa, reminding her of the impromptu shower the two college friends had held in her bedroom.

They'd given her frilly nighties made of the silkiest fabric. She'd never had anything so lovely. She hadn't wanted to tell them she was getting married because of Wade's kids. Neither had he. In fact, they hadn't told anyone the truth, not even the kids.

"It's a private matter between us," Wade had insisted. "Let them think whatever they want. I want the kids to believe we're going to be a normal family, that their world is as secure as every other kid's in this town."

She'd agreed because it made things so much easier. The problem was, even on her wedding day, Clarissa still wasn't sure what "normal" was in their case. He'd said she was pretty a lot of times. And lately his arm had taken a liking to her waist, especially if she left her hair down.

It made her breath catch when his fingers trickled through the strands and he compared it to silver in that muted growly voice. She'd learned a little about his family, too. His mother had been a silversmith. At least, she wanted to be, until her husband deserted her and she had to waitress to make ends meet.

Clarissa pushed the reminders of romantic dreams away as she felt heat rise in her face. If he hadn't said it, lately Wade's kisses had shown he found her attractive. But what did that *mean*?

This was still a marriage for the children's sake. No matter how much she wanted to pretend, Clarissa knew that romantic love had very little to do with it.

Mrs. McLeigh poked her head around the door, her round face beaming. "Come along now, dearie. The music's just starting. You follow your friends down the aisle, and then Bertie Manslow is going to sing something or other. I forget the name of it. Then the reverend will get busy and marry you two love-birds. All right?"

Clarissa felt a surge of panic and held out a hand. "No! Wait."

"Prissy? Honey, is anything wrong?" Briony's soft fingers covered hers.

Clarissa dredged up a smile as nerves twitched her stomach around like a little boat on gigantic waves. "No, I just need a moment to compose myself. You know, pinch myself to make sure it's real. Can I do that?" she asked Mrs. McLeigh, who'd designated herself wedding coordinator and organized the entire community into sponsoring what seemed to be the wedding of the year.

"Oh, of course you can, you sweetheart! Out you go now, ladies. Into the powder room. Let's give the bride a few moments. It won't hurt her groom to cool his heels."

Blair stayed where she was frowning, but Clarissa patted her hand reassuringly. "I just want to pray a minute," she told her, smiling away her fears. "I'm fine."

Blair's face cleared. "I'll pray too," she whispered back. "But I think God's already done His best work putting you two together."

"Thanks." But as she sat alone in that room, listening to the organ music, Clarissa closed her eyes and prayed desperately for reassurance. Was this the right thing to do? Was she making an awful mistake? She'd tried so hard to build bridges between herself and Wade, even asked his uncle to be part of the ceremony.

"Ah, there you are." Carston Featherhawk slipped inside the room after one quick knock, his mouth slashed wide in a grin. "Time to walk the beautiful bride down the aisle. Wade's a lucky man to have you take him on. 'Specially with all his trouble. I just hope he's learned his lesson. Not like last time."

"Last time?" A niggle of fear grew by leaps and bounds. Clarissa stuffed it down. "What do you mean?"

"Never talks about himself much, does he?" Carston nodded. "Can't say as I blame him. Had a pretty tough life with his dad leaving like that. Like to killed my sister to find out he'd just dumped her and the kids and walked away. But she stuck to it, got herself a job and devoted herself to Kendra and Wade. Wasn't her fault her man couldn't handle his duty to the family. Ran away, he did. Just when Mary, my sister, needed him most."

His mouth tightened, his eyes grew cold. "She killed herself caring for that boy, and what did he do? Just like his dad. Up and left her to face the music on her own when she got sick." Carston stopped, then frowned as if he'd only just realized to whom he was speaking.

"It's all right. We're going to be married. I should know this, I think." Clarissa wasn't sure that was altogether true, but it was too late to back out now. She wanted to know all about Wade, but she'd never been able to coax any of his past out of him. Was this why?

"I suppose, being as you two are about to be wed, you should know the worst." Carston nodded, scratched his chin again and then plunged into the past. "Wade was always a wild one. Hated it when the other kids made fun of him, his clothes, his race, his drawing. Learned to fight young. He'd get a rebellious streak in him and nothing could stop him from fighting. Once he busted up a house and then ran away. Mary cried herself to sleep for days, aching for him to come home. When he did, he acted as if he'd never done a thing wrong. Don't suppose he ever paid her back, either."

"Wade ran away?" Clarissa wanted to get this clear.

"Sure, lots of times. Made it a habit, you might say. Always wanted his own way, did Wade, even if it cost somebody else. He's the one who got Kendra killed, you know." He tsk-tsked at her white face. "Oh, not directly, of course. But it was his fault, all the same. He's to blame and that's the truth."

Clarissa's heart dropped to her shoes. Wade had never spoken to her of Kendra except to say that she was his sister, the kids' mother and that she was dead. Was this why? Because he felt guilty? But for what?

His uncle was saying Wade ran away from trouble. Was that what he would do at the first sign of problems in their marriage? Clarissa didn't kid herself that there wouldn't be any. All marriages had problems. Especially ones based on a lie, and she had lied when he'd asked her if she thought their friendship would carry them through.

She didn't, because she was counting on building more than a friendship with Wade Featherhawk. That's what she'd prayed for every night for the past two weeks.

"I'm just gonna get me a drink of water," Carston muttered, licking his lips. "Then we'll get this shindig on the road. I think you'll be real good for Wade. He needs a strong dependable woman to keep him on course, make him face up to reality."

After Carston left, Clarissa closed her eyes and groaned. Was that what she was? Some kind of a rudder! It was not what she wanted from her marriage.

Here I am, on what should be the happiest day of my life, and all I can think of are questions.

What if things got hard, very hard, and Wade ran away from his responsibility—her and the children? What would she do then?

"Pray," Clarissa reminded herself, wishing Carston had delved into this before today.

What should she do now? The whole town had gotten into the spirit of their wedding, donating flowers, decorating the church, sponsoring a shower and a reception, even arranging for a short honeymoon at a nearby campground.

If she didn't go through with it, she'd be a laughingstock. Again. Not only that, Wade's business would suffer. She wouldn't be able to tell them why she opted out, of course. How could she say she had doubts? They thought she was deliriously in love with him because that's what she'd wanted them to think so they wouldn't pity her! If she dumped him on their wedding day, the whole town would speculate and the awful rumors about him would surface once more. Could she do that to him? To the kids?

I've got to start this marriage with trust. I don't know what happened back then, but I know Wade now. I've seen his love and devotion to those kids. And I know he's committed to our marriage. He won't let me down.

Clarissa gathered up her bouquet, straightened her dress and pushed her shoulders back in determination. She'd wished and prayed for a husband and a family. The answer had come. Now it was up to her to fulfill her part of the deal.

I won't be a burden, she promised silently. *Not like with Gran. I won't ever make him feel that I can't carry my own weight in this family. I'll make him see he doesn't need to feel responsible for me, to give up anything for me.*

The door burst open and Carston stood on the threshold grinning. "Ready?"

Clarissa took a deep breath, whispered one more prayer for peace, then nodded. "I'm ready," she murmured.

"Good! 'Cause those kids are like to popping their buttons outside, waiting to parade down that aisle. I don't think I've ever seen so many attendants in a wedding." He folded her arm in his and led her into the vestibule, his voice soft with pride. "Wade's a lucky fellow. Getting a second chance doesn't happen for everyone."

Clarissa ignored the shiver of worry his words ignited. She chose instead to concentrate on Tildy with Jared, then Lacey and Pierce, gliding down the aisle in the measured step Blair had shown them. Next came her closest friends, Briony and Blair, wearing their soft pink gowns.

Finally it was her turn. She glanced toward the front just once and caught sight of Wade, standing beside the pastor in a black suit that fitted him to a *T*. She saw his eyes widen in wonder at his first glance of her in her grandmother's wedding dress. It was a Ginger Rogers style gown with layers and layers of sheer white silk falling away from the tiny pearl-studded bodice. It was the one thing Gran had left behind that Clarissa didn't harbor the least bit of guilt in accepting.

Clarissa felt elegant, beautiful, desirable for the first time in her life. And it was all because of the very tall, very handsome groom who stood waiting for her with that crooked smile and that glittery look on his face. Was he as nervous as she?

Clarissa met Wade's uncertain smile with one of her own, then nodded at Carston. "I'm ready," she whispered and stepped out.

This was right. This was good.

This marriage would last. She just had to do her part.

"It was a nice wedding. They must think highly of you to have gone to so much work." Wade tugged his bow tie off and tossed it into the back seat of her car. "I intended to change before we left, but somehow I never got time."

She knew what he meant. All those last minute

instructions for the kids had taken eons. But Bertie Manslow had insisted that the bride change into her going-away outfit and then toss the bouquet. Clarissa still wasn't sure how it came about that Blair caught the huge sheaf of purple-blue spring iris. Could she have been thinking about her own cancelled wedding and about the fatherless little boy who waited at home for her?

"That's quite an outfit, by the way. It's very…" he thought for a moment. "Elegant," he finally said.

"It is a little overdone, isn't it?" Clarissa fingered the red shantung jacket with its neckline of frills. "But since it was a gift and I'll only ever wear it this once, I suppose it doesn't matter."

"Oh." Wade drove on, obviously unsure of how to continue the conversation. "Are you hungry? You didn't eat much of the mountains of food they laid out."

"I was too busy talking to everyone, I guess. It was kind of them to arrange it all." Clarissa sighed, slipping her feet out of the stiletto heels that pinched, to rub them in the soft carpet.

"I can't understand why anyone would ever *want* to go through that again." Wade shook his head in disgust, his voice telling her he certainly hadn't enjoyed it.

Clarissa felt the prick of tears and ordered herself to be sensible. "I'm sorry you didn't like our wedding," she said in a small voice.

"No! I didn't mean…aw, shucks! I've spoiled it again, haven't I." He huffed out a sigh that told her reams about his state of mind, and in particular, his opinion of this wedding. "I can't seem to say anything right today. I just meant that it was so busy. All those people, all those gifts to open! It seemed, well, overdone. Too busy. More like a public spectacle.''

"I'm so sorry. *If* you wanted a more private wedding, you should have said so. They've waited a long time to see me married. I guess they wanted to do it right. Especially after Harrison." She was about to explain more about Harrison, but Wade cut her off.

"I do not want to hear another word about your first fiancé. I got an earful of him already." His voice didn't encourage her to continue. Neither did his face. It might have been chiseled from granite.

Her heart sank. Here they were, only hours married, and already they were arguing. She swallowed hard. *Don't be a burden on him, don't weigh him down with your problems or he'll hate you for it.*

"I'm sorry, Clarissa." The gruff apology barely carried over the boisterous voice of the radio deejay.

Without asking, Clarissa reached over and shut off the annoying sound. "It doesn't matter," she muttered, surreptitiously brushing away a tear.

She turned her head and stared out the window, wondering how and when this day would end. Her nerves were stretched so tight, she wanted to scream, but grabbed a handful of red shantung instead. "It really doesn't matter."

With a muttered epithet, Wade pulled over to the side, out of traffic, and brought the car to an abrupt halt.

"Yes, it does matter." He shut off the engine, then reached out a hand to press her shoulder so she would turn around. "The only way we're going to make it through this is to be truthful with each other. We can't hide our feelings. Agreed?"

She nodded, but kept her eyes downcast.

"I liked the wedding. I especially liked your dress. You looked beautiful." His right hand brushed across her hair, fingers rubbing it between them as if it were a fine silk.

She heard the funny catch in his voice and wondered why it was there. "It was my grandmother's wedding dress. She always said she'd wanted my mother to wear it, but my parents eloped. I don't think she would have minded." Her own voice came out in a breathy whisper, but Clarissa ignored that because her heart had just speeded up to double time.

The fingers on his left hand closed over hers in a squeeze, then opened and threaded through hers so their hands were interlocked. She could feel his plain gold wedding band pressing against her knuckle and automatically rubbed at her own.

"It was gorgeous...*you* were gorgeous." A tiny laugh came from low in his throat. "I guess I'm a little nervous. I've never been married before."

"Neither have I." She risked a glance up at him, and found him gazing down at her with a quizzical stare. "It was pretty rushed, wasn't it?"

He shook his head slowly, his eyes burning into her with a steady flare glowing in their depths. "No. Actually it was perfect. All of it. You did a wonderful job."

There was something in his voice, something she didn't understand. But she couldn't look away from him.

"Actually, I didn't do any of it," she babbled in

a rush. "It was mostly Mrs. McLeigh...." Her voice died away, the words stuck in her throat. Nothing would come out when he kept looking at her like that.

"Clarissa?" His voice dropped to almost a whisper.

"Yes?"

"I'm going to kiss you."

Clarissa blinked. How did she answer that? "Oh."

"Do you mind?" His mouth moved nearer, his lips very close to hers, his breath, sweetly scented with the chocolate from their wedding cake mixing with the tang of the punch they'd toasted each other with.

Clarissa took a deep breath. "No," she whispered. "I don't mind." She held her breath and closed her eyes as his mouth came down and grazed across hers. "Not at all."

"Good." There was the sound of laughter in his voice. "Then would you please kiss me back?"

She looked up at that, her eyes widening as she saw the caring in his face. He wanted this day to be special for her! That knowledge eased her fears and she slid her hands around his neck, nodding as she did.

"I'll try. Though I'm not very good at kissing." Yet, she amended silently. "But I can learn."

Then Clarissa kissed him with all the pent-up emotion she'd kept so carefully in check during the many times their lips had met during the reception. This time there were no observers, and she tried to put her feelings for him into actions rather than words.

If she was a little confused about exactly what those feelings were, well, he didn't need to know that.

When the kiss ended, Wade's hands dropped away from her with obvious regret.

"Is something wrong?" she whispered, aghast at her own nerve in kissing this man.

"Yes," he nodded. "Something is definitely wrong with my brain."

"P-pardon?" She straightened her jacket and pushed her hair back, conscious of the fact that he'd loosened the entire mass so badly that she couldn't possibly get it back in order without a mirror and her brush.

"I must be nuts to be sitting here on the side of the road, kissing you with the whole world watching us."

He jerked a hand toward the window and only then did Clarissa see the interested spectators craning their necks for a better look. Wade rolled his eyes, shook his head and then grinned at her ruefully.

"Shall we, Mrs. Featherhawk?" he asked, almost playfully.

"We shall." She joined in without a second thought. "Drive on, Mr. Featherhawk."

After that it was simple to stop for dinner at a small wayside restaurant, to find the campground where a cabin had been rented in their name, to drive through the overhanging boughs of spruce and cedar to a small log building nestled between two massive pines.

"It's really lovely, isn't it?" Clarissa stood on the porch and looked around at the beauty of God's world shown to best advantage in the clear moonlight and a few strategically placed lights. ''How kind of them to do this for us.''

She gasped when his hands caught her up against his chest, barely managing to stifle the shriek that would have alerted the other campers, wherever they were, to their presence.

''What are you doing?'' she whispered loudly as he struggled to reach the doorknob. She leaned down and unlatched it with her free hand. The other one refused to move from its anchoring position against his neck.

''Carrying you over the threshold. Isn't that what you were waiting for?''

''No!'' Clarissa gasped as he lowered her to her feet, her face burning with color. ''I never even thought of such a thing.''

''Well, I want to keep up with tradition,'' he mumbled, his face darkening. ''Isn't that what all the hoopla was about earlier?'' Then he turned and went back out the door.

Clarissa blinked and tried to pretend that she didn't wonder if he was coming back. But her sigh of relief when he staggered in the door with their cases gave her away, if he'd been paying attention.

Which he wasn't. In fact, as he closed the door on the cabin and surveyed the rustic interior, Wade tried to convince himself that he hadn't noticed anything about his new wife at all. That project was not a success.

The gold band on her finger gleamed as if she'd spent the ride here polishing it. Her hair, loose and flowing down her back, just begged to be brushed until it once more resembled the sheet of burnished silver-gold that he'd glimpsed so many mornings. And that suit of hers—that blazing red drew attention like a fire engine.

Wade didn't like what he was feeling. None of it. He wasn't a family kind of guy. Deep down the stark truth was that Wade didn't believe in families. He sure as shootin' didn't believe in his ability to manage one. He'd only done it out of necessity.

Maybe he should have told her that? Yeah, right. Before or after he kissed her?

"Is anything wrong, Wade?" Clarissa studied him with a tiny frown that pleated the porcelain skin between her elegant brows. "Is something the matter?"

"No. Yes. Uh…" Wade shook his head in disgust, trying to come up with a way to tell her. "That is, maybe you'd better sit down, Clarissa. There's something we need to discuss."

"All right." Her voice was quiet, almost frightened. As if she expected the worst and needed to steel herself for it. She sat down across from him in the overstuffed recliner that almost swallowed her delicate body whole. Her hands settled primly in her lap, her chin tilted upward to receive the blow. "Go ahead."

"It's not anything bad," he muttered, mentally kicking himself for spoiling the ambience. She deserved better. He forged on. "It's just that I wanted us to understand one another right off."

"You don't have to tell me, you know. I am quite aware that this is what is called a marriage of convenience. And I'm quite willing to take the sofa." She forced a timid smile to her lips, obviously striving to pretend that the little quaver in her voice wasn't there.

"It's not just that." He flopped onto that sofa, squeezed his eyes closed and desperately searched for the right words. They weren't there. "I'm not a family man, Clarissa. I'm too selfish, I guess. I spent a lot of time watching my parents' marriage fail, and while it did I was responsible for my sister. I didn't want her to see the ugliness when they were fighting, to hear the awful words."

Clarissa nodded as she listened. "That's perfectly natural," she murmured, her head tilted to one side. "As a big brother, you must have been a wonderful friend."

He shook his head. "Not really. I made her play the games I wanted to. She had to fall in with my wishes, because I was in charge. But that's not it." He chewed his lip in frustration. Why was this so hard to say? Wade thought for a moment, then started again.

"I hated the responsibility of it, you see. I wanted *them* to look after her, to make sure she was okay. There were so many things I wanted to do and she got in the way." He shook his head. "I messed up so many times. Once I made her eat some berries and she was sick for a week." One hand raked through his hair as he remembered her thin body shaking with the fever. "Anyway, my dad left. Uncle Carston probably told you that?"

She nodded.

"It was pretty rough then. I was the man of the house, but I did a lousy job of looking after my mom and Kendra. I couldn't wait to dump them onto somebody else so I could go after my own dreams.'' He stopped abruptly when he realized where this was going. No way was he digging into that now. He straightened his shoulders, drew in another breath and continued.

''Let's just say it wasn't any paradise. After Kendra got married, I finally felt free. I made up my mind then and there that I would never be tied down to anyone again. I never wanted the responsibility of someone else's happiness.'' He tried to read her. ''Do you understand what I'm saying?''

''Yes, of course.'' Clarissa nodded, her eyes clear and calm. ''You don't want to be accountable for my problems. You took the children on because you promised your sister, and you've done the best you could with them because you figured it was your duty. But it's not the life you would have chosen for yourself. Close enough?''

She didn't get it, not all of it anyway. But she was pretty close. Wade nodded slowly, rephrasing his thoughts. ''Well, yes, but...''

She held up a hand. ''Oh, I'm not finished yet. I'm not stupid, you know. I understand exactly what you're saying, Wade Featherhawk. You think I'll add to your responsibilities, that I'll be even more of a burden on you. And you're scared stiff. Is that about right?''

Wade gulped. Meek and mild little Clarissa Cartwright, no Featherhawk, had a lot more on the ball than he'd given her credit for. Now she'd made him feel like a jerk, which he probably was, for wanting to live his life without thinking about anyone else.

''Not scared, no.'' He couldn't let that go. ''It's

just an awful lot for me to handle at one time, Clarissa. Four kids! Nobody has *four* kids in this two-point-five-family world. If they do, they get them one at a time!'' He groaned at the selfish words that poured out of his own mouth.

I sound like a wimp. Wade shoved his head into his hands and dragged at the roots, trying to realign his topsy-turvy world.

"I love them, Clarissa. I do! But it's hard to go from being independent to being a father of four, and then a husband. It's gonna take me some time to adjust, that's all I'm saying." That sounded better, didn't it? As if he just had a few issues to work through and then life would be rosy.

If it wasn't the way he felt, she didn't need to know that. After all, Clarissa was taking them all on and she wasn't even related! She was going to have to adjust far more than he.

"What I'm trying to say is, don't get too upset if I'm not very good at this. I'll probably need a lot of practice before I come anywhere near being the kind of husband you deserve."

She laughed at him! Wade could hardly believe that light, tinkling sound that shattered the tension in the room like a high note splintering a crystal goblet. He stared, frowning at the smile curling her lips.

"It goes both ways, Wade. I've never been a mother or a wife and now I've got to get used to all of you at once. At least you had months to train." She got up and walked over to sit beside him. Her hand patted his. "I promise I won't expect too much of you," she said quietly. "We'll learn as we go along. But please, don't feel you have to be responsible for me. I'm an adult. I can look after myself. I can look after you and the kids too, if you'll let me.''

Relief, pure, unadulterated relief washed over him. He didn't have to be some kind of Superman or Romeo for her. She knew and understood. God had worked a miracle in this woman.

Wade leaned down and brushed his lips across her cheek. ''Thank you,'' he whispered with heartfelt emotion. ''Thanks for understanding.''

She nodded, then got up and moved toward the other rooms. ''Let's have a look around, shall we? Then I wouldn't mind going for a walk. I need to breathe fresh air.''

Wade managed to maintain her light-hearted approach to life for the rest of the evening. He made fishing jokes, teased her about leeches in the lake, insisted she take the bedroom and he the couch.

But late that night as he lay staring through the patio doors at the big moon outside, he wondered if he should have told her all of it. Maybe he should have made sure she knew that he would never love her.

Maybe Clarissa should know he couldn't afford to love anyone. Not anymore. Everyone he loved died because he was too selfish to care for them when they needed him. Their pain was always his fault. It was also his secret.

Chapter Five

On her very first morning of being Mrs. Clarissa Featherhawk, the bride decided to set the tone of her marriage as she meant to carry it on.

She wanted to know Wade better, certainly. She craved the personal details that all couples learned after months of courtship. But she didn't have that basis of information to rely on because Wade seemed to think he had to protect himself. Or perhaps he wanted to protect her. She wasn't sure. Her only hope lay in calming his fears, showing him that she intended to be an equal partner, that she had no intention of dragging him down.

Which was why, tired as she was from the busy day before, she managed to drag herself out of bed as the first threads of sunlight drifted across the sky. By the time she noticed Wade stirring from his uncomfortable position on the sofa, Clarissa had cinnamon buns ready to emerge from the oven and coffee, freshly brewed in a big mug on the table beside his makeshift bed.

"It can't be morning yet," he grumbled, his tousled head emerging just above the back of the sofa. "I've only had my eyes closed for ten minutes."

"Rough night?" she murmured, turning away to hide a smile when she saw him force his eyes apart. "There's a cup of coffee by your elbow. Maybe that will help."

"Maybe," Wade muttered doubtfully, but he downed a mouthful just the same. "What are you doing?"

She turned to find him frowning at her, one eyebrow quirked upward in a question. Her cheeks grew warm under his steady regard.

"I was just making some buns, before the day got too warm. This year has been a strange one, hasn't it? You never know if you're going to fry or freeze." He was still staring at her. "Anyway, I thought it would be a good idea to do this before the cabin heated up too much. I've got our dinner started in that Crock-Pot."

"Dinner?" He blinked twice, took a gulp of coffee, then winced as it burned down his throat. "I didn't realize you were so industrious."

Clarissa wanted to pinch herself. How stupid of her! Of course. He wanted to sleep in and she'd disturbed him.

"I'm sorry," she muttered, transferring one of the buns to a small plate. She kept her eyes averted. "I'll just pour myself some coffee and go outside. I didn't mean to disturb your rest. Go back to sleep if you want. I'll sit in the sun and read."

He muttered something in that low husky rumble of his, but Clarissa didn't hang around and listen to what it was. She scurried out the door like a frightened mouse and carried her breakfast to the edge of the lake where earlier that morning she'd set out two of the chairs from the veranda.

"So much for romantic dreams," she scolded herself. "Just get on with your life and quit expecting it to change. It's a marriage of convenience, girl. Not a love match."

She'd known that, of course. But still the foolish dreams had filled her mind last night. Those teasing "maybe" dreams. Maybe one day, maybe if they got to know each other, maybe somehow she could be a real wife, a real mother.

The sun rose slowly, its warmth spreading like fingers across the tree strewn landscape, rippling over the lake on butterfly wings. Birds drenched the air with their song. The put-put of a motorboat echoed the presence of a fisherman out early to cast a line.

Clarissa closed her eyes, tipping her head up to let the sunshine chase away the doubts. "Lord, I thank You for this wonderful creation. And for Wade. I know Your hand was in this marriage. 'All things work together for good.'" She stopped a moment to wonder what life would be like in another five years. The murmuring sounds of other campers drew her back to the present, and she hurried on with her prayer.

"I want to do my part, to be all that You want me to be. But I don't know what to expect, what Wade expects. Please give me patience and strength to wait on You." She opened her eyes, her attention riveted on the man who'd just stepped outside their cabin door. She'd have to hurry.

"And God, if You could make him care about me, just a little bit, it would make this marriage so much easier." She breathed a sigh of relief. "Thank you, God. Amen."

Wade flopped down in the chair beside hers, his bare arm brushing against her hand where it held her coffee mug out of harm's way. "This place is like an isolated piece of solitude in a messed-up world," he told her, his eyes on the trees sparkling in the bright sunlight, their reflection shimmering in the smooth lake water. "In a way, I guess it reminds me of the reservation, though there wasn't much solitude there. In fact, when I lived there, I felt as if nobody else knew I existed."

Clarissa saw through the undertones to the pain he tried to mask. "Abandoned, you mean?" she murmured softly, keeping her gaze on the water. "I know what that's like. When my parents died and I went to Gran's, it was as if the life I'd known died. Gran was wonderful, of course," she rushed to assure him. "But she was older, and she'd just lost her only child. I didn't want to impose."

She could feel Wade's eyes on her. "It must have been tough."

Clarissa nodded. "It was. Maybe that's why I can empathize with your kids. In one split second, everything you've ever known is changed and you can't ever go back." She took a deep breath, crossed her fingers, then plunged in to something she had no business questioning. If she was going to learn more about Wade, this was the time.

"You must have felt that way when Kendra died and you had to take over for her. Your plans, dreams, hopes for the future. They all had to be put on hold, didn't they?" She hoped he'd tell her what those hopes and dreams were. She hadn't expected his mocking chuckle.

"Snooping, Clarissa?" He caught her chin and forced her to meet his glinting stare.

Clarissa knew he could see the round spots of embarrassed color that burned in her cheeks but she didn't back down.

"Yes, maybe just a little. I'm hoping I can learn to understand you and the kids a little better, get to know what your lives were like then." She refused to look away. "Is that wrong?"

He stared at her for a long time before his hand fell away from her jaw and he sighed, a deep huff that told her he would give just so far and no further.

"No, it isn't wrong. It's normal, I suppose. What do you want to know?"

Clarissa groaned inwardly. This wasn't what she wanted. She wanted him to open up of his own accord, to share a piece of himself because he could trust her. Maybe it was too early for that.

Please help me, Lord.

"I want to know anything you want to tell me," she murmured, wishing she could smooth away the lines of tension around his eyes. "What were you like as a little boy?"

Clarissa settled back in the chair and drew her knees up to her chest, smoothing her skirt over her legs to hide from the prickles the sun was already making against her skin. Thank goodness she'd thought to tug on the old straw hat she'd found. That along with her long-sleeved shirt should give some protection. She didn't want to go home looking like a boiled lobster!

She turned to nod at Wade. "I'm listening."

He shook his head wryly. "Don't give up easily, do you?" His eyes darkened, then glassed over as if he'd gone far away, to a place where she couldn't go. "What was I like? I was a brat, Clarissa. Disobedient, willful, argumentative. All the things you were probably instructed not to do—" he raised one eyebrow, then continued when she nodded her understanding "—I did them. All of them. There wasn't a younger kid I didn't terrorize, a teacher I didn't sass back, a rule I didn't break."

"Problem child," she murmured, more to herself than to him. But he heard it and nodded, his face drawn.

"Worse." He summed it up succinctly. "I'm sure you can't possibly understand."

Her lips smiled, but inside her heart ached. "Can't I?" She remembered the times she'd cried herself to sleep, begging God to bring her parents back so they could be a family again, promising anything if He'd just stop punishing her.

Wade frowned as he watched her, his eyes inquisitive. "You couldn't. You've had the perfect life."

"Have I?" She pleated the fabric between her fingers, noting the glossy pink polish that Bri had applied just yesterday morning was now chipped. Sort of like her dream of blissful married life. Clarissa decided it was too ironic to dwell on. "Don't get sidetracked so easily by what you see, Wade. Truth is sometimes hard to find.''

He inclined his head. "I guess. Anyway, it got worse when the fighting got worse. My parents couldn't agree on what side to butter the bread. They sure couldn't compromise on raising Kendra and me. Dad got fed up and pretty soon I figured out that if you were out of sight, you were out of mind. I made it a point to be out of his sight as much as possible.''

The wealth of understatement in those words drew tears to Clarissa's eyes. She wanted to say so many things, to comfort Wade, tell him she understood. But more than anything, she wanted him to continue talking. She made herself be satisfied with touching his arm as she whispered, "I'm sorry."

He didn't turn her way, but his head jerked in acknowledgment.

"My mother, bless her, never gave up on me even though I disappointed her so many times. She wanted me to have all the things she'd missed and to her, that meant living on the reservation, learning about my heritage." He grimaced. "All I could see was that being an Indian and loving a white man had made her life a misery. She didn't fit into his world, and he sure didn't fit into hers. I fit into neither. I was determined to get as far away from there as I could, to find something better."

"So that's when you ran away?" Clarissa laid her head on the back of her chair, her fingers light on the bunch of muscles that clenched and unclenched as he spoke.

"Yes, I ran *away*, but I thought I was running *to* something. I just couldn't figure out how to find it.

When I was seventeen, I finally ran far enough that I ran into someone who showed me there was more to life, if I was willing to take it. His name was Ralph Peterson and he was an artist, a good one. He picked me up when I was hitchhiking, took me in and kind of adopted me for the two weeks I was gone. He showed me the places he'd sketched, real and dreams, places he could draw on a piece of paper. Places so wonderful they took your mind off your problems. He had a house full of pictures—buildings and places around the world. I was hooked on those cathedrals, castles, temples.''

"So you decided to become an artist?''

"Not really. I just got more and more curious about the process of how you got a building from a picture. When the police brought me home, I spent every spare moment I could find at the library. I read about Frank Lloyd Wright, I studied the styles and I started to sketch.'' He made a face. "You can imagine how that went over—a macho male sitting around drawing! I got into a few fights over it.''

"I'd like to see your drawings sometime,'' she whispered, aching for the almost-man who'd searched so hard to find himself. "You have a real talent with building things, so I'm sure that's where it came from.''

"Thank you.'' He paused a moment as if reflecting, then his face hardened. "I was awful to Kendra. I was so focused on what I wanted, what I had to have, that I couldn't see that she was upset by the parents, too. She needed someone to talk to, but I wasn't there for her.''

"Wade, your parents had that responsibility. Not

you. You were a child. You should have had the freedom to dream.''

He shook his head, his mouth tightening into a bitter line. "She was my sister and I was so selfish I wouldn't even let her use my stuff." He puffed out a scornful half laugh. "I'd decided, you see, that I was going to make myself into somebody the world had to notice, that people were going to sit up and pay attention to Wade Featherhawk. I was too good for the reservation, too smart for my mother's plans and too old to bother with Kendra. As soon as I could, I took off and got a job, construction. I learned as I went how to do a good job. Kendra and Mom seemed okay then and I'd work away summers. Then Mom died.''

Clarissa nodded. She knew this part. "And you had Kendra.''

"Yeah, I had Kendra. There wasn't anybody else. My dad had disappeared and the folks who wanted her were bad news. It was up to me, and I hated being the one dumped on." He swallowed, his voice choked but insistent. "You had to know Kendra to understand how loving she was. It tears at me even now when the kids look at me in a special way and I see her. She didn't care if I was rich or famous or not. She loved me. All the time. No matter what.''

"I guess that's what sisters do." Clarissa let the silence stretch between them as he remembered his sister's joy.

"She was such a happy kid. Always chattering a mile a minute. I loved her so much. But I didn't dare take her with me to the sites. We lived in bunkhouses a lot of the time. She was young and gorgeous, and the men I worked with weren't the type for her to be around.''

Clarissa could tell from the hard chiseled lines his face had fallen into just what kind of men he'd worked with and was fiercely proud of the way he'd protected his sister.

''I tried to take care of her as best I could, but I had to leave and find work whenever we ran out of money. She'd stay with some friends.'' His voice dropped to a whisper. ''She'd throw her arms around me when I got back and hug so hard my ribs ached.''

''She loved you.'' Clarissa felt the sting of tears for that young girl burn in her chest.

Wade looked up. ''Actually, you remind me of her sometimes. She wouldn't take no for an answer, either. She was soft but so stubborn.'' His eyes glinted reproof.

Clarissa grinned. ''You have to stand up for something or you'll fall for anything,'' she teased.

He nodded slowly. ''She should have stood up to me,'' he muttered.

Clarissa wanted to ask why but he began speaking again.

''The building industry went into a slump right after I finished high school, and I couldn't find work. I didn't know what to do. I only had sixty-five dollars when I came home. I was scared stiff to tell her I'd have to leave again so soon. And I was fed up with grubbing along, just barely managing.'' His fingers fisted until the knuckles grew white.

As Clarissa watched, he slowly straightened each finger, his jaw hard with the discipline of stifling his frustration. ''She was so young and so innocent, I couldn't imagine her leaving the reservation, getting a job. Then I had a better idea. Why didn't she marry Roy? He'd been chasing her for years, she'd be eighteen in a couple of weeks. Everything would be wonderful.'' He smiled but there was no joy in his face. ''Or that's what I thought.''

''It wasn't?'' Clarissa couldn't stop herself from reaching out and feathering a hand through his hair, brushing it back, her fingers soothing against his scalp. ''It sounds reasonable.''

Wade shook his head, leaning back so her hand fell away. It's as if he can't bear to accept kindness, she decided. As if he has to lash himself over and over with his faults.

''It was grasping at straws and I latched on to that one for all I was worth, eager to get rid of my burden. That's what I thought of her. My own sister was a burden I had to get rid of.''

The recrimination and self-loathing she saw in his eyes tugged at Clarissa's soft heart.

''I could hardly wait to be free of my own sister. Isn't that sick? I had all these dreams of what I was going to do if I could just be on my own. I'd begun to earn my high school credits. I knew the college I wanted. Big man on campus, that's who I wanted to be!''

''There's nothing wrong with that, Wade. You were just trying to plan ahead.''

''Yeah. That's what I told myself, too. I had to dump her on the first guy she liked for her own best interests. Because I couldn't be bothered hanging around that reservation. *I* had to be free to find my dreams.''

There was nothing she could say. Nothing that would obliterate the sorrow he carried inside. All she could do was help him understand that God still loved him, as He loved them all in spite of their shortcomings. She whispered a prayer for guidance, then concentrated on Wade's next words.

"I should have checked him out more, come home more often, paid attention to her letters. When she finally got hold of me in California, her life was a mess. Her marriage was on the rocks and her husband was dumping her and the kids, just like good old Dad." He shoved his head into his hands, his fingers tugging on the glossy strands of black.

"But did I get her out of there, even then? No! All I could see were my selfish plans going down the tubes, my life getting put on hold, my dreams unfulfilled." He kept his head bowed, his face averted. "I hurried home to talk her into trying to make it work, just a little longer. Just until I got what I wanted. That way, I could avoid my responsibility to take care of my sister. It was the one thing my mother made me promise I'd do and I failed her. Again."

Wade's face was carved into hard lines when he finally shifted in his chair, his bitter gaze pinning Clarissa where she sat.

"Kendra died in that car accident because I sent her there. She didn't want to go with Roy, he'd been drinking. But I persuaded her that she could make it work if she just persisted. It's my fault those kids have no father or mother." His eyes shone like polished iron, his mouth tight.

"So you tell me, Clarissa. Am I the kind of person

you want to be married to, the kind of man you want making decisions about your future?''

He lunged to his feet, his eyes blazing. ''Don't bother to answer. I know you only wanted to help the kids. So do I. You probably think they'd be better off without me messing up time and time again. You probably wish I'd take off for good and leave them in your capable hands.''

His voice dropped to a whisper as he turned away.

''And I would. God knows I'd leave in a minute if I could. But I promised her I'd raise them. It's the last promise I ever made to her and I can't break it. I just can't.''

Clarissa sat stunned and immobilized by the heart-rending grief that shredded his voice. She wanted to reach out, to assure him that he was doing the right thing.

But was he? Were they?

She watched him walk around the lake, a lonely solitary figure lost in a brooding silence that clearly stated *Keep out*. When he disappeared into a stand of towering blue spruce, Clarissa let the tears roll down her cheeks.

''Oh, God,'' she whispered, ''what have I done? How can I help this hurting family?''

Though she sat there for an hour, the answer evaded her. Eventually she got up, picked up her and Wade's empty mugs and returned to the cabin. She cleaned it, made some sandwiches for lunch and set a fresh jug of iced tea in the fridge. But Wade did not return.

As she lay at the side of the lake later that afternoon, Clarissa forced away the thought that Wade had run away, left her behind. Not this time, she told herself. He's committed this time. And I intend to see that he doesn't feel chained down. I'll go on with my life as usual and he'll realize that I've accepted him for exactly who and what he is. He won't have to fulfill my expectations because I won't have any.

She pulled off her cover-up and stretched out on the towel, allowing the hot sun to touch her sunscreened skin.

"'They that wait upon the Lord,'" she reminded herself. "Your timing is best."

"You're going to burn if you stay out here much longer." Wade's soft voice broke through her dream, the words tentative. "Maybe you should cover up?"

"I think I'll try the water first." Clarissa sat up, surprised to see him clad in his swimsuit, a towel looped over one arm. "Are you going in?"

He nodded. "I love swimming. The colder the better. We used to have an old swimming hole...." His voice trailed away. "Never mind."

Clarissa let it go. "Well, I'll try," she mumbled doubtfully, accepting his outstretched hand as she got to her feet. "But if it's cold, I'm outta here."

He tilted up one arrogant eyebrow. "I never thought I'd see the day when Clarissa Cartwright would back down from a challenge," he teased.

"Featherhawk," she reminded him. "And I'm not backing down. I'll go in. And then I'll get out."

He rolled his eyes when she tentatively toe-touched the clear water lapping against the white of the beach. "Uh-huh. Chicken. That's what I said."

Clarissa could feel the tension in him, knew he

was trying to lighten things between them. Very well. She would help him. She untied her beach jacket and tossed it to the sand, then dashed into the water.

"Last one in is the biggest chicken," she bellowed, then gurgled as she stepped off a ledge and the icy water closed around her sun-heated body and filled her gasping mouth. "Oh!"

"You live on the edge, don't you?" Wade's big hand wrapped itself around her arm and tugged her toward shore. "You don't have to prove to me that you're brave, Clarissa. I'm the guy you married, the fellow whose four crazy kids you took on. Remember?"

"I remember." She hugged herself tightly, arms wrapped around her middle to conserve what little warmth still pulsed through her body. "Since you already know how brave I am and that I'm not a chicken, c-c-can I get out n-now?"

Wade threw back his head as he roared with amusement at her chattering teeth and shaking lips. Gently he led her out of the water, wrapped her beach coat around her and wrapped his own towel around her dripping head.

"You don't back down, do you, lady?" he said, admiration lacing his voice.

Clarissa gathered her stuff into her bag and headed toward the cabin, fully aware that Wade was right beside her. "Feel the fear and do it anyway," she mumbled. "That's my motto."

They walked toward the cabin and up the steps. At the top, Wade reached out a hand and stopped her. His eyes held a quizzical look that she couldn't quite decipher.

"Sometimes fear is a good thing, Clarissa. It makes us stay away from situations where we can get badly hurt." His dark eyes bored into hers.

She held his gaze. "And sometimes hurt teaches us things we wouldn't have learned if we hadn't stepped out in faith, believing that God is always in control. 'If God is for us, who can be against us?'" she quoted softly.

His hand dropped away, his face a study in conflicting emotions.

"I'm going to change," she told him finally.

He nodded, wet hair drooping into his eyes. He slicked it back, his eyes on her. "In that bag of tricks, have you hidden the ability to cut hair?"

She winked. "I can cut it." She shrugged. "It might end up a little shorter than you like, but I can cut it."

He nodded. "That's what it's all about, isn't it? Trying." He opened the door. "After you, Mrs. Featherhawk."

She curtsied. "Thank you, Mr. Featherhawk."

As beginnings went, it was a start. A good start.

Chapter Six

As honeymoons went, Clarissa didn't think it ranked among the most romantic, but she'd enjoyed it more than she'd believed possible three days ago. They spent their time hiking around the lake, sunbathing, dipping their toes in the frigid water and talking.

She knew he liked beef, didn't like three-piece suits and was a master at both sketching quirky little pictures and avoiding talking about himself. She told him about her grandmother's dutiful raising of her, the freedom she'd found at college with Briony and Blair, and her friendship with half the town.

They'd figured out an accounting system for household needs. Wade argued that the children were left enough money for their needs, though he admitted that he'd tried to hoard it for the college educations their mother had wanted.

Wade refused to allow Clarissa to chip in more than a minuscule amount to the budget, insisting that he would cover the improvements they made to her house. He was her husband, he would also be her provider. She didn't like that, but he ignored her argument and she'd eventually given in to prevent further debate. Which didn't mean she wasn't going to let him pay for everything. After all, she had some pride!

He held her hand when they sat by the campfire at night, even kissed her again. And she kissed him back. But those occasions were few and far between. On the whole, they'd spent their time as good friends might, which was rather a nice way to begin.

In fact, by the time they were sharing the return drive to Waseka, Clarissa felt quite comfortable in this new relationship. Sure, she wished for more. Who didn't? But every night she reminded herself that God had given her far more than she'd ever dreamed of. It was up to her to be happy with that.

"Have you got anything special lined up for this week?" he asked, turning off the highway onto the narrower road that led into town.

"No. I thought it would be enough to get used to everyone for the first little while. Anyway, the kids will be finished school soon and there will be all kinds of outings before that." She had a list of them in her purse. Picnics, trips to the local forestry farm, the usual end-of-year school field trips.

"I thought it might be nice for them to go to summer camp, even if it's only for a few nights. What do you think?" She waited, anticipating his negative response.

"Summer camp?" He frowned. "Isn't that kind of expensive?"

"Not the church camp, no. They have scholarships if you need them. Or the kids can earn a deduction on their fees if they bring someone." She whispered a little prayer for help before listing the benefits. "I thought going might get them to interact with other kids a bit. It's kind of the norm around here and they need to start settling in, feeling secure in their place here."

He shrugged, lips pinched tight. "I guess. I was sort of hoping to take them camping myself. I promised them a long time ago that I would, but I've never done it. Kendra probably could have used the break."

She heard the self-condemnation in his tone and ignored it.

"Family camping! What a good idea. We could go back to the lake." She fell into a daydream of the six of them splashing in the water, building a campfire at night, forming the bonds that made a family secure. And one day, maybe, just maybe...

"We're home. Oh, boy!"

Clarissa jerked back to reality at the amusement in his voice. She stared at the huge banner that decorated the front gate. *Welcome home Mr. and Mrs. Featherhawk.*

"I'm afraid that's probably due to Blair," she told him with a sigh. "She always loved plastering signs all over our room at college."

"I wonder what else she's encouraged. It was nice of her to stay with them, though." Wade helped her out of the car, then followed behind her with their suitcases, his voice filled with amusement. "She really steps in and takes over, doesn't she?'' He motioned toward the newly enlarged flower bed.

I've got to make sure he doesn't feel overwhelmed by all of this. Clarissa made a mental note to have supper on the table when he came home at night. The house would be spotless, the children organized. Wade would only see the benefits of having married her. She would make sure he didn't feel hemmed in or burdened with his wife. Far from being a responsibility, she intended to become an asset he couldn't lose.

''They're here!'' The shriek of joy came from Pierce. Seconds later the door flew open and all four of the children bounded outside and down the stairs. ''Welcome home.''

''My, what a welcoming committee! You all look like you've grown six inches.'' Clarissa hugged each of them in turn, marveling at this family she'd been gifted with. ''You've done wonders, Blair! You'll probably need a month-long rest.''

''No way! I know all about the demands of motherhood. Remember?'' Blair winked, reminding Clarissa of her young son who'd stayed at home. She hugged her close, then leaned back to survey her friend of ten years. ''Is that a tan you've started, Prissy?''

Clarissa blushed. ''If it isn't, it's not for want of trying.''

''Well, good for you. You look great. Marriage agrees with you. Both of you.'' She made no bones about hugging Wade, too, then ushered everyone inside. ''Come on, supper's ready. And then I've got a flight to catch. Daniel wants his mommy back.''

They giggled and laughed all through the meal. It wasn't until Wade left to drive Blair to the airport that disaster struck unannounced.

"Come and see, Clarissa. We've fixed your room up."

She smiled and followed them up the stairs, only to stop, aghast, at the entrance to her bedroom. The room was the same, yet it was totally different. Her little vanity desk still sat there, but next to it, the chiffonier had been cleared of its photos and a host of male paraphernalia lay on its polished surface. Her closet had been altered to accommodate Wade's jeans, chambray shirts and one good suit. In the adjoining bathroom, his electric razor lay beside the collection of perfume bottles she'd assembled from her grandmother's stash.

"He's going to need that razor." Jared chuckled from his position on the edge of her canopy bed. "He didn't shave the whole time, did he?"

"No." Clarissa didn't know what else to say. It was obvious that they expected her and Wade to inhabit this room together. And why not? Didn't most couples sleep in the same bed, in the same room? How could she tell them otherwise without opening a new can of worms?

Better to let Wade deal with it when he returned.

"What is that heavenly fragrance? Don't tell me the lilacs finally opened?" She whirled around searching, then stopped as she spotted her grandmother's crystal vase filled to capacity with a mass of the tiny deep-purple blooms. "Thank you, children! This is just lovely."

She hugged each of them again, taking care not to

muss Tildy's new, rather precarious hairdo. Only Blair could have sprayed that much goop on it and left someone else to get it out.

"We thought we could watch a video together. You know, kind of our first night together?" A flicker of doubt washed through Lacey's young eyes. "Or maybe you'd rather not."

Clarissa instantly changed her mind about shooing everyone off to bed. Sure, they needed an early start for church in the morning. But they needed time with her and Wade more. They needed time to assimilate the new family that they were now part of.

So did she. Lots of time before she climbed these stairs and shared her most personal space with the man she'd married such a short time before. She grabbed on to the diversion like a lifeline. "That's a lovely idea! What's the movie?"

They trooped down together, each child vying for the important part of telling her some tidbit about the show. Clarissa laughed.

"Sounds to me like you've already seen this. Why do you want to see it again? And why don't we wait for Wade?"

They fell over each other trying to explain how long he'd be and how great it was and, rather than crush their joy, she joined in with the fun.

"All right, all right! We'll watch it. How about some popcorn to go with those sodas?"

By the time Wade returned, they were settled in and Clarissa had tears rolling down her cheeks at the plight of the little boy on the screen.

At the kids' urging, her husband flopped down on

the sofa beside her, flicking away a tear from her sad face. "Really enjoying this, are you?" he teased.

She nodded, smiling at him through the mist. "It's a wonderful show," she sobbed.

"Shh!" The kids' eyes were riveted to the screen.

Wade shook his head, took the can of soda she held out, and grabbed a handful of popcorn. "I'd hate to see it when you *really* like a movie." He winked, then focused on the movie.

Caught up in the plot, Clarissa thrust the bedroom issue to the back of her mind. She'd tell him about it later, she decided. After the movie. When the kids had gone to bed.

They were all weeping by the time the credits rolled.

"Man, it's good to be home. Nothing but happy faces to greet me." Wade surveyed the mass of soggy tissues Lacey clutched in each hand and sniffed in sympathy.

But Clarissa knew he wasn't unaffected by the trauma the family had suffered, or by the happy ending when everyone had been reunited.

"Oh, stuff it!" She pretended to tap him on the shoulder, then turned to the kids. "It's pretty late. I think you'd better get to bed."

They put up no arguments, merely bid her and Wade good-night, kissed each of them and trundled up to the rooms they'd taken over after the fire. There was some good-natured squabbling, of course, but nothing serious.

Clarissa had just breathed a sigh of relief that they'd left her in private to explain the bedroom situation when Pierce came rushing back downstairs.

"I hope you like the room, Uncle Wade." A huge grin split his face. "Evan North told me you're supposed to put cornflakes in the bed after people get married but I didn't do it. There wouldn't have been enough for breakfast."

Wade's lower jaw was approaching his chest, so Clarissa stepped in. "That was very kind of you, Pierce. It would be pretty hard to start a morning without cornflakes, wouldn't it?" She smiled and patted his back, knowing how much the boy treasured his favorite cereal. "If you don't mind, I think I'd like to show Wade your handiwork. Is that all right?"

"Sure. 'Cause you're married now, right?" His big eyes moved from one to the other of them with something like satisfaction glowing in their depths.

"That's right. Good night." She ruffled his hair, hugged him again, and gave him a little push toward the steps.

"Yeah. Okay. Night." He stopped for one last look, grinned, then raced up the stairs.

"Bedroom?" Wade peered down at her curiously. "What's that all about?"

She pulled him into the kitchen and let the door swing closed. After checking to be sure no one had come back down the stairs, Clarissa cleared her throat and launched into an explanation.

"They thought it was the thing to do, I guess. And actually," she hesitated, then blurted out, "they were right. I don't have another empty bedroom. Not since you made one into an office anyway."

He stared at her for a long time, his eyes dark. She knew he was trying to come up with an excuse, a way out. She knew because she'd tried the same thing. There wasn't one. Not unless he wanted to tell the children the truth.

"I thought I'd let you decide what to do," she murmured.

"Oh, thanks! I should tell them we got married, not because we love each other, but because of them. That we thought they needed a stable home, that we had to get married or they would end up in foster care?" He shook his head determinedly. "I don't think so, Clarissa. It's not even an option."

"So, what will we do?"

"I don't know." He poured out another cup of coffee, tasted it, then dumped the entire pot down the sink.

"It's been there since supper. Shall I make you a fresh cup?" She fluttered around, tidying up the kitchen. "Wade?"

"What? No. Thanks." He shoved his hands in his pockets. "I think I'll sit outside for a bit. Maybe something will come to me."

"Good idea." She followed him out, sank into the chair opposite his and tried to pretend she wasn't staring at him. "Blair got off all right?"

"Fine. On time. Said she'll call you tomorrow. I was supposed to give you some kind of message." He frowned, rubbing his temples as he tried to remember. "You owe her? I think that was it. For when it's her turn, I think she said. Her turn for what?"

"Her turn to get married." Clarissa explained about their college pact, formed after they'd been dumped at the altar, or rather, just before it. "We decided that if one of us eventually did get married, there must be hope for the others. Wade—'' she peered at him through the gloom ''—we perpetuated the myth that we were in love with each other and Blair bought it. Just like the kids.''

''Yeah, just like the kids.'' He huffed out a sigh, then leaned back in his chair and studied her. ''I know it's an imposition. It was supposed to be for public, not for private. But if you think you can handle having me sharing your room, I'll try not to get in the way.''

She saw his eyes jerk away from hers and study the floor. And then Clarissa knew just how much he hated having to ask.

''I don't know what else to do. I want the kids to feel secure and I'm afraid that if word got out why we were married, Rita would renew her campaign. As it is, we still have to be approved to adopt them.'' His eyes narrowed, dark and intense. ''Is it too much to ask that we share? Just for a while. I promise I'll try to respect your privacy as much as I possibly can.''

Clarissa gulped. He was going to share her room? He was going to be there, every morning she would wake up and see him. Every night she'd go to sleep knowing that he was right there. Even someone as naive as she was knew it was asking for problems!

But what else could they do? She'd promised to help him however she could. She'd also promised not to be a burden. This was one way of making his life a little easier.

And satisfying this silly craving to be near him that

you have. She stifled that mocking voice and summoned a smile.

"Of course we can make it work. And I'll respect your privacy, too. I'll do the very best I can, Wade. I promise."

"Thanks." He sighed, his shoulders sagging.

Suddenly Clarissa knew how worried he'd been. And she felt a thrill of pleasure that she'd been able to do this for him. She cared about Wade. And about the children, of course. After all, God had sent them to her. She was sure of that. So it was her duty to make the best of this awkward situation.

"I think I'll go up to bed, if you don't mind locking up?" She tried to think of how she could make it easier for him to fit in. After all, it was already her home. She wanted him to feel as if it were his, too. "Come whenever you're ready."

"I'll just sit here for a bit. You go ahead." He didn't bother with the customary peck on the cheek she'd received for the past three nights. Instead he stared off into the darkness as if it held the remedy for the frown that marred his handsome good looks. "Good night, Clarissa."

She couldn't think of anything else to say, so, finally, she turned away, went inside and slowly climbed up the stairs. She unpacked quickly, then prepared for bed by having a shower, shampooing her hair and drying it with the blow dryer, brushing her teeth until her gums bled, and applying the moisturizer she'd bought in Hawaii and never touched again. And as she did, she listened for his footstep.

But when she came back into the bedroom, Wade still was not there. Clarissa lifted off the white satin wedding ring quilt her grandmother had made to match the canopy, folded it and laid it on top of her grandfather's army trunk. She turned the lights off so that only a small lamp burned on the nightstand on Wade's side of the bed.

He wasn't coming.

The knowledge stabbed deep into her heart. She was so homely that he couldn't stand the thought of sharing her room, let alone this huge bed with his own wife. But then, she wasn't really his wife, was she? She was just going to be the mother of his adopted children.

Clarissa snapped out the light and curled up in the bed. She said her prayers, then huddled up into a little ball, as close to the edge of the queen-size mattress as she could get while hot tears trickled down to soak her pillow.

"This isn't what I wanted, Lord," she prayed. "But You know best. I just have to wait on You."

It seemed as if it was only minutes later that the bedroom door flew open and a chorus of four happy voices chanted "Happy Mother's Day!"

Clarissa blinked through the curtain of hair that covered her face, trying to convince herself that it really was morning. Ow! Something sharp—an elbow poked into her ribs. Why would an— Wade! She sat up with a jerk, fully awake now as she dragged her hair off her face and swallowed.

"Uh, thank you," she managed, edging as far away from him as possible. It was a little embarrassing to have to tug her arm out from under his and his foot was on the corner of her long flannelette nightgown.

Lacey was the first to speak, her voice hinging on tears, her eyes bright. "We know you're not really our mom. She died with our dad in the car accident. But we thought, since you married Wade, and he's looking after us, well…"

"She means that we'd really like to have you for our stepmom. Or aunt." Pierce frowned, scuffing one toe against the carpet. "How does that work, anyhow?"

"It works however you want it to." Clarissa risked a sideways glance at Wade, who'd managed to draw himself up against the headboard. By the look of him, he hadn't slept any better than she. "We just want to be here for you whenever you need us. Right, Wade?" She looked at him full on, waiting.

"Yeah. Right. Of course." He finally came to enough to comment. "What's on that tray?"

"It's for Clarissa. For Mother's Day. From all of us." Tildy carried the tray forward and carefully set it on Clarissa's lap. "I hope you enjoy it."

Clarissa lifted the soup bowl that covered the plate and made herself smile at the runny concoction that oozed out all over the plate. "Scrambled eggs! And look, Wade. There's bacon, too."

"And toast. I made that." Jared preened a little bit. "It's your day so we wanted to make it special."

"You've made it very special," Clarissa told him, feeling teary at the effort and thought they'd obviously put into this. "Thank you for the kind welcome to the family. I really appreciate it, guys."

They stood there, four children who'd lost the

most important people in their lives, and grinned at her as if she were the best thing to happen since sliced bread. Clarissa felt proud all the way to her heart. These were her kids now. Hers and Wade's. And she owed them her very best effort at mothering.

"Hey, not bad!" Wade had reached out and was now sampling one of the blackened strips of shriveled-up bacon. He licked off his fingertips and tilted his head. "Where's mine?"

"Uh-uh. You get to come and help us clean up the kitchen," Jared told him. "This is Mother's Day. Not Father's Day."

"Oh. Right. I can hardly wait." He waved a hand toward the door. "Out you go and let Clarissa sample her breakfast in peace."

"But we hafta see if she likes it!" Pierce frowned at his uncle. "It's important."

"It's delicious. I don't know when I've tasted better." Clarissa gulped the forkful of egg down, ordering herself not to gag as it slipped and slithered down her throat.

"It's nice not to always eat your own cooking, isn't it?" Tildy laid her hand on Pierce's shoulder. "Come on. If you'll help me clean up, I might even make you pancakes." In mere seconds she had them out the door, pulling it closed behind her.

"I think I'd better go supervise. I'd hate to think what she could do to pancakes." Wade shuffled out of bed and toward the bathroom. He stopped and turned around suddenly, his eyes glinting with wicked humor. "Do you want me to dump that before they get back or are you going to play the martyr and make yourself sick eating it?"

Clarissa held up the tray. "I love those kids, but I'm afraid I can't bear this sight any longer. Please, do the honors."

He walked back, picked up the tray and popped the bacon into his mouth as he headed for the bathroom. "Actually, this isn't bad. If you like your bacon crisp. Really, really crisp."

Clarissa straightened her gown while he was out of the room and pulled her hair back into some kind of order. "I did drink the juice," she called out in self-defense. "And I sampled the toast."

He plodded back into the room and set the tray on the night table. "Which one was the toast? That black cardboard stuff with the lines on it?" He grinned at her. "I thought maybe they were coasters or something. And where's the coffee? Nobody has breakfast without coffee."

"Don't suggest it. Please? I shudder to think what might happen to my delicious mountain-grown blend."

He sniffed, eyes winging up to the canopy. He frowned, his eyes busily studying the frills and flounces. "It's all mountain grown, Clarissa. There isn't any other kind of coffee."

"Oh." She yawned and laid back down, tugging the covers up to her chin. "You can have the bathroom. I'm going back to sleep."

"How can you dare?" he demanded. "Don't you realize they're down there, running rampant all over this house? Life as you know it may never be the same again."

"Oh, it's not that bad," she mumbled, closing her

eyes as she snuggled against the pillow. "They're good kids."

"Yeah, they are." He stood there staring down at her. "Clarissa, about that canopy—"

She hid her smile. It hadn't taken him long. She stretched her neck and peered upward at the ornate, totally feminine concoction her grandmother had insisted was perfect for a young girl. "What about it?"

"Well, no offense, but it's not me." He scratched his forehead, then fingered the quilt on the chest. "Nor is this. Feels like satin or something."

"It is."

He jerked his hand back as if it had been burned, his eyes huge. "I can't be around satin."

"Why? Are you allergic?" Clarissa shifted into a sitting position. She wasn't going to get back to sleep now.

"Allergic? I guess you could say that. I'll wreck it, Clarissa. Look at that, I've snagged it already." He balled his hands into fists. "I work around sawdust and stuff. I'll get everything dirty. My hands are rough. I'm not used to all this frippery."

She giggled. "If it makes you that uncomfortable, I'll replace it. But you haven't ruined it, Wade. It's just a thing. A nice thing, true. A gift from my grandmother. But it only has meaning because it came from her. We can always get another bedspread, if that's what you want."

She wouldn't tell him that she'd really wanted a bedroom with flowers, blue flowers. And a bedspread that didn't show every bit of dust. It seemed ungrateful when Gran deserved all her gratitude for the sacrifices she had made.

"You don't mind?" He sighed his relief, then jerked a thumb upward, crossing his pajama clad legs. "What about that? Can we change it, too?"

Clarissa faked perplexity. "Change the canopy? Why?"

"It's a girl bed, Clarissa." Wade looked pained by the words.

She pretended to scratch her neck so she could hide a smile. "Of course it's a girl bed. I'm a girl!"

"I know *that*." He sounded strange, as if he were being tortured. "It's just…oh, never mind. I think I'll go have a shower."

"Okay. I'm going to sleep a little longer. Wasn't it nice of them to think of making this a Mother's Day for me?" She snuggled down. "They're wonderful kids, Wade." She was almost in dreamland when his softly mocking voice penetrated her brain, his breath brushing against her temple as he whispered against her ear.

"Yeah, they are. Wonderful little dears. So why do I have this mental picture of your house in ruins?"

"Oh, boy!" In a flash she was up, had her robe wrapped around her and was flying down the stairs. Sure enough, the bottom floor of the house was filling rapidly with smoke. In fact, the smoke alarm began to whine. "Tildy? What are you doing?" she called, opening windows as she went.

"Don't come in here!"

The words stopped Clarissa outside the kitchen door. "But there's smoke all over. I have to come in."

"No, you don't. Anyway, there's no fire now. I put it out."

Clarissa's closed her eyes. "Oh, Lord, please help me," she whispered.

"Uh, Clarissa?" Tildy's voice came through the thick wood.

"Yes?"

"Do you think you could get Uncle Wade and send him in here? It's, uh, kind of important." There was a certain urgency in Tildy's voice that transmitted through the swinging door.

Clarissa wheeled around and raced back up the stairs. She pounded on the bathroom door, and when there was no answer, shoved it open and stuck her head inside. Steam filled the room.

Wasn't that great? Smoke all over the bottom floor. Steam all over the top. Or there would be soon if he didn't shut off the hot water. And what was that awful caterwauling noise?

Clarissa shoved it all to the back of her mind and bellowed for all she was worth. "Wade?"

He stopped midnote, pulled back a tiny corner of the shower curtain and peered out. "Is something wrong?"

"Yes. There's smoke all over downstairs, and Tildy won't let me in the kitchen. She says you're to come right away."

She heard the water shut off, winced as something fell to the floor, then blinked at the yelp of pain. "What's wrong?"

"Somebody keeps turning on the hot water, that's what's wrong. I'm almost frozen, the parts that didn't get scalded the last time, that is!" He sounded very grumpy indeed. "You need a temperature regulator."

Clarissa frowned. "Do I?" She had no idea what a regulator was. "Are they expensive?"

There was a long drawn out sigh. "Look, Clarissa, I'll explain it all to you later, okay. Right now, would you mind leaving this bathroom?"

From the top of her head to the souls of her feet, Clarissa felt herself burn with the mortification of it. It spread through her body like a poison ivy rash. How could she have stood here, yakking like that!

Married four days and she was acting as if she had every right to be standing in the bathroom while Wade took a shower. What must he have thought of her? She gulped. No time to think about that while the house burned.

"Yes. Yes of course. Naturally. Right." She backed out of the bathroom as fast as she could, and jerked the door closed just a touch too forcefully. It didn't stay closed, of course. It never did when you banged it like that.

But without a backward look, she scurried out of the room, down the stairs and found the farthest corner of the sofa in the living room to crunch down in.

What was wrong with her? She'd actually enjoyed the camaraderie of it! Before she'd realized what she was doing, of course. For the first time in years, aside from the odd occasions when Blair and Bri had come to visit, she'd woken up feeling safe and no longer lonely in that huge bed.

"Oh, no!" She squeezed her eyes closed as the idea birthed inside her brain. "It isn't possible. It's silly, stupid, schoolgirlish. I'm too old for it." But it wouldn't go away.

"How could I possibly be falling in love?" she whispered. "It was supposed to be an arrangement that benefitted everyone." She tested the idea out loud. "Do I love Wade?"

It didn't sound bad at all. In fact, there, cuddled up inside her heart, it felt snug and secure, like a little pilot light that burned steadily and wouldn't go out. It didn't matter that she'd only known him a short while. The problems, the kids, the differences in their backgrounds and expectations, none of that mattered a whit.

She was falling for her husband!

Clarissa grinned and hugged herself with the sheer joy of it. She'd known it would come, had known she'd find it one day. It was just as Gran had said, love came when you least expected it. It kind of sneaked up on you, grew inside until it was ready to bloom.

She sat there and reveled in it without paying the least attention to the strange noises from the kitchen. Who cared about kitchens? She loved her husband.

Clarissa fell to dreaming about all the wonders that awaited her in this marriage. There were so many changes she wanted to make, in herself and the house, but also for the children and Wade. She wanted this to be the perfect family, the perfect marriage. And it would be if she worked at it.

But out from under all that joy, a nasty little voice poked its head up and reminded her of the facts. They were hard to acknowledge and they rubbed the glow off her discovery. Wade didn't love *her*. In fact, he'd already told her that love was out for him.

He didn't believe in families and the forever kind of love that she'd waited for for so long. To Wade, this marriage was just a necessary step in the care and feeding of his nieces and nephews. He'd made a promise, he'd stick by it. He sure didn't want or need Clarissa fawning over him, uttering protestations of love.

She bowed her head as a tear worked its way out of her eye and plopped onto her folded hands.

"Father, did You give me this family, these wonderful children, and Wade, just to take it away again? How am I to be a wife to him if he won't let me past that barrier he keeps up? If he won't let me in, how can I love him? How can he learn to love me when he won't talk about what's wrong?"

Silence.

And then the piercing truth dawned. She'd asked God for a husband and a family to love. Hadn't He sent both? So what if Wade wasn't exactly the kind of husband she wanted, the children weren't either her biological children, or the fluttering little cupids she'd imagined?

She'd married Wade knowing the facts. He'd made it abundantly clear on their wedding night that he never intended to fall in love. She'd agreed to take on the kids because they were wonderful children and they deserved a chance to grow up happily with their siblings around them.

But how can it possibly work when I love him so much? Wade doesn't want responsibility, he doesn't want to be tied down to someone like me. He just wants a mother for the kids, a friend and companion. He doesn't need another encumbrance.

In a split second the decision was made.

She would never tell him of her love. She would play her part, do what he needed done, but she'd love him secretly. And if the folks in the community saw the truth, they wouldn't be surprised since they'd assumed she'd married for love.

"I've got to do it, don't I, God? I've got to go on with what I started, keep my promise." Some of the chill that surrounded her dissipated a little and a remnant of warmth snuggled around her heart. "Okay, maybe I didn't get all of my dream, but I got the best part and I'll love all of them the very best I can."

What if he leaves you like he left them?

No sooner had that thought crossed her mind than she remembered Paul's letter to the Philippian church when he'd told them to be full of the joy of the Lord.

"Don't worry about anything; instead pray about everything; tell God your needs and don't forget to thank Him for your answers."

"I won't worry about it. I'll leave the answers up to Him. He is *God*, after all. He can do anything." Saying the words out loud made them more real, more official somehow.

Clarissa closed her eyes and poured out her heart to her heavenly Father, telling Him her heart's desires. By the time Wade came to find her, she had brushed away the tears.

"Are you okay?" he asked carefully.

"I'm fine. Why?"

He shrugged. "Just wondered. She didn't wreck

anything this time. Just dumped the entire bowl of pancake batter on top of the stove. I cleaned it up, but—''

''—it's going to take a while to get it back to normal,'' Clarissa finished for him. She burst out laughing. ''Who cares? As long as everyone is all right, that's what matters.'' She felt the joy she'd prayed for bubble up inside. ''Kids will be kids.''

He tilted his head to one side, his eyes bright. ''You're a wonder, Clarissa Cart—Featherhawk. I wonder if I'll ever understand how your brain works.''

She got to her feet, brushed a kiss across his cheek, then walked to the door.

''You will if you practice, Mr. Featherhawk. It'll probably take about, oh, forty or fifty years of marriage before that happens, but you can do it.''

He blinked. ''That long? What goes on underneath all that hair anyway?''

She giggled and raced up the stairs to get ready for church.

''You'll find out,'' she promised as the shower hissed over her. ''You certainly will find out.''

Chapter Seven

"I'd love to give him the message, Mr. Chapman, but he hasn't come home yet this evening. Mm-hm." Clarissa shifted from one foot to the other uncomfortably. It was so hot, and she was so tired. Why had Tildy picked today to bake?

"They're trying to finish up the golf club, so every moment counts. I'm sure he'll get to your garage door as soon as he can. But if you can't wait, I know Wade will understand if you have to hire someone else. Actually, it would be easier on him, too. His list is so long." She listened to the protest with a tiny smile curving the corner of her lips, then rang off thoughtfully.

Over the past six weeks, the remarks about Wade's heritage had died down until almost everyone in Waseka wanted him for one odd job or another. His workmanship was top-notch, though Clarissa felt his prices were a little low. She intended to speak to him about it, if he ever showed up before she was asleep and stayed until she was awake. The only way she knew he'd been there was the stack of laundry and the wet towels he left behind.

"I don't think it's a good idea to tell them it's all right to go elsewhere, Clara. I need those jobs to pay the bills."

She jumped at the sound of his low voice, then whirled around. "I wish you wouldn't sneak around like that. I almost dropped the teapot." She inspected his dear face and winced at the lines of tiredness around his eyes. "Are you going to finish in time for the grand opening on Saturday?"

"Of course." There was nothing but exhaustion in the words.

"You don't have to push yourself so hard, Wade. The people here know you do a good job. You've got them lined up until Christmas, according to my list." She held out the sheet on which she'd compiled the incoming calls. "I only gave approximate dates because I didn't know how long each project would take. You'd better look it over while I get you something to eat. Is a salad platter okay? I fixed fruit salad for dessert. The kids are upstairs. Asleep, I hope."

He flopped into a chair and began unlacing his boots. "I don't need anything. I'm too tired to eat anyway."

She ignored that and began pulling things out of the fridge. "Nonsense. You have to eat. You're working yourself to the edge as it is." Clarissa smacked the plate on the table in front of him, poured out some of her freshly made iced tea and added six ice cubes.

Wade ignored the food, long enough to take a huge gulp of the tea. "I'm fine, Clara. Don't fuss."

"Fuss?" she sputtered. "I haven't begun to...why do you call me that? Clara?" The indignation died away to curiosity. "That's the second time you've said it."

"Well, it's better than Prissy, which is what I heard Blair call you." His eyes dared her to deny it. "Anyway, that's how I think of you. Kind of like an old-fashioned character in one of those musty books you're always reading. Heidi maybe, only older and without pigtails." He began eating automatically. "You know the kind I mean. They look stern on the outside, but you know very well that deep down they're made of mush. The kind that need protecting."

Clarissa stared. She hadn't known he thought anything about her, let alone what she was like underneath, in her soul.

"I don't need protecting," she said after a long moment, intent on making him understand. She sank down into a chair across from him. "I am exactly what I seem. Tough. Durable. Able to handle any knocks life dishes out."

He chuckled, his eyes dancing as he surveyed her scrunched-up body, folded like a pretzel into the chair. "You have got to be kidding! Look at you, sitting there in that white sunsuit thing, as elegant as if you stepped out of one of those magazines Lacey likes. You haven't got a hair out of place."

She huffed. "That's because I just had a shower, silly. I was in the garden after work and I got filthy. Then Jared needed me to help him with the mower, and we had to take some stuff apart. I wasted a huge amount of water trying to get the grease out from under my fingernails, you know.''

"You tackled the lawn mower?" Wade picked up her left hand and studied the perfect ovals, now tinted a pale-pink shade. "Yes, this delicate little hand is definitely that of a laborer," he grinned. Then his face sobered. "It's far too hot for you to be working outside. Leave the gardening to Joe Franklin. He said he'd do it for you."

She yanked her hand away, frustration mounting. "You're not listening to me, Wade. I'm *not* some delicate flower. I *like* gardening and I *want* to do it myself. I have been for years. Besides, I know more about that motor than Joe ever will.'' After prevaricating for a minute, she finally decided to get out all the frustration that had mounted during the past weeks.

"This is supposed to be a partnership, remember? I have a job, I want to contribute to this family, too. I'm not some anemic little hothouse flower you have to take care of. We're partners. If you'd just tell me a little bit about how you do things, I could handle some of the book work, too. I'm good with numbers.''

He shoved the half-eaten plate away, red-rimmed eyes suddenly blazing. "Along with managing a house full of four demanding kids, sewing the girls special outfits for camp, mending Pierce's terminally torn jeans and working full-time, I suppose?" He shook his head in disgust. "You should have let me get someone to stay with them during the day, instead of having them come to you at the library."

"Wade, they *help out* at the library. And they get paid for it, courtesy of the town, not me. It's good for Jared and Pierce to be able to earn their own money. Tildy has that job helping Mrs. Simmons with the baby every morning, and Lacey is busy with vacation Bible school at the church. We're doing just fine!"

He jumped up so quickly, his chair upset with a crash. Wade ignored it, stomping around the table to circle her wrist with his thumb and fingers.

"Fine? Look at you—you're skin and bones! You haven't had a moment to call your own in weeks and you keep taking on more. Why can't you let me be the breadwinner in this house?"

In a flash, Clarissa's frustration hit white-hot. She jerked her wrist out of his hold and jumped to her feet. "You *are* the breadwinner! You're gone night and day, working yourself into an early grave so that you can prove you're doing your duty by the family." Temper took over her brain and she forgot to pick her words carefully.

"Do you think having a few extra dollars in the bank means anything to Pierce when you missed his first Little League game? Or to Tildy when she won that home ec award at school last month? They just want you to share their successes. Way down deep they don't care if you buy them a better bike or brand-name shoes."

His hands came up to fasten onto her shoulders in a steely grip. "I can't just walk off the job whenever there's something they want to show off," he growled. "I'm the only one they have left. I have to make sure they're taken care of."

I'm the only one they have. Clarissa wrenched her body out of his grasp. White-hot indignation rose inside, and a shaft of pain pierced her heart.

"Well, silly me! I thought I was in their lives, I thought we were together in taking on this responsibility. Sorry for being concerned. And I am *not* a bag of bones! I can't help it if I'm just naturally thin."

Clarissa saw the frown roll across his face like a thundercloud and knew she'd blown it. She turned and flew up the stairs to her bedroom, hot angry tears flooding down her cheeks as she carefully closed the door so the children wouldn't wake up.

Ohh! She could spit she was so angry. After all this time, he was still keeping her out, refusing to share his life with her. Why did he keep doing that, insisting that he would take care of everything, as if he alone were responsible for how the children grew up? Didn't their marriage mean anything to him?

"Clarissa? Can I come in?" He stood in the doorway, his shoulders slumped with exhaustion as he waited for permission to enter their bedroom.

The utter weariness on his face touched a chord deep in her heart, but Clarissa couldn't forget his earlier words. She wanted to share and he wouldn't.

"Why not?" she mumbled at last. "It's supposed to be your room, too. Even though you're never here."

She sat in front of the mirror and pretended to ignore him, though she knew the exact moment he stepped through the door, closed it and advanced toward her. To hide her nervousness, she reached up and pulled out the pins securing her French knot, letting her hair fall down around her shoulders.

"Stop that, Clarissa, and listen to me!"

His voice barked out harshly, and she let her hands drop away, frowning as she turned around to study him.

"I'm sorry. I didn't mean to yell at you, but I need you to pay attention to what I have to say." He crouched down in front of her, took her hands in his, and held them. His voice was soft but a thread of tension wove through it. "I don't want to argue with you. God knows I've had my fill of arguments and I don't intend to do that in my marriage."

"Arguments aren't always bad, Wade," she murmured, enjoying the feel of his work-roughened hands on hers. She leaned forward to look directly into his eyes. "Sometimes they get the truth out so people can deal with it instead of a lot of silly pretense."

"You think that's what I'm doing? Pretending?" He frowned. "About what?"

She decided to be candid. "About this marriage, about this family, about my role in it and yours." Clarissa drew a deep breath and plunged in. "About what would happen to this family if you slowed down and took a look, a good look at who we really are."

"Who you are?" He dropped her hands as if they burnt him, then backed away to perch on the edge of the trunk, his mouth drawn in a line of bitterness. "I know exactly who you are. You're the person I drew into this mess. You're the person who is stuck caring for four kids that are my responsibility, one which I've dumped on you. I don't blame you for being angry.''

"I am not *stuck,*" she blurted out furiously. "I love those kids. And I am not angry. Well, maybe a little.''

He continued on as if he hadn't heard. "But I promise that I won't take off and leave you with them, Clara. I know that's what you've been afraid of ever since my uncle blabbed about the past.'' His eyes met hers steadily. "I'll do whatever it takes to make sure we don't drain you of every penny you earn. Put your own money somewhere safe, somewhere you can draw on when you want to retire.''

"My own money? I thought it was ours.'' Clarissa stood, defeat dragging at her now, when she'd felt so much anticipation just an hour ago.

"You're not listening,'' she told him sadly. "You won't hear what I'm saying. I married you because I wanted to help you and those kids find a way to stay together. And I wanted to be a part of it. I thought I could make a difference in your lives, that I could be part of something wonderful.''

Wade stayed where he was, staring at his toes. Clarissa decided they had to start somewhere and she might as well be the first. She took a deep breath and dove in.

"I never had a family, Wade. Never had a sister to chum around with, or nieces and nephews to play with. I only ever had Gran. She was a wonderful woman, but she wasn't what you'd call warm or loving. She had a strict sense of her duty and she intended to do that duty by me, come what may.'' She swallowed the lump in her throat and continued.

"You have no idea how much it hurts to be the person someone else is responsible for. You lose your freedom to be spontaneous, because you're afraid it will cost them something else. You're afraid to say what you really think because maybe they'll feel they gave up more than you deserved. You're afraid to get mad because maybe they'll hate you and then where will you go? You live your life in a tight little box of restrictions, knowing always that your indebtedness can never be paid off."

Wade said nothing, merely stood there frowning at her.

"I won't live like that anymore, Wade. I won't let you make me live like that. I am a part of this family because I care about the people in it, and because I have something I can and *want* to give." She walked across the room, took his chin in her hand and forced his eyes to meet hers.

"When I've given too much, I'll let you know. Until then, don't try to smother me with your false sense of duty. And don't protect them so much they can't fly."

"I—I—" He stopped and shrugged. "Go on. Finish what you have to say."

"I'm an adult, Wade. I am responsible for myself. And with you, I'm responsible to raise those children. I'll let you know if I need your protection, but I'm telling you right now that they need you around. You can't make their lives perfect, you can't make sure nothing bad ever happens again by killing yourself with work. You can't make up for the past."

Tears came then, but she brushed them away. She stepped forward and wrapped her arms around his waist. She laid her head on his chest and said the words she'd waited so many nights to say.

"I'm sorry Kendra's gone. I know you felt responsible for her, for the kids losing their mother. I'm sorry you hurt. But you can't bring her back with guilt. They need to talk about her with you, to remember the past, good times and bad. They're strong. They can deal with it. Can you?"

Wade's hands automatically moved to wrap around his wife. He couldn't have stopped them. He wanted to hold her, to squeeze her so tightly, to bind her to him in a way that would prevent her from ever leaving.

Yet, what she was saying hurt so much.

"What do you know about Kendra's death?" he muttered, his chest tight with the stabbing pain of bringing it all into the open again.

"Nothing. Only what you've told me and what I've seen on your face. I hoped you'd tell me about it. The children won't speak of it because they think it hurts you too much. Pierce keeps a little book under his pillow and every time he remembers something happy about his mother, he writes it down, so he won't forget her." Her eyes begged him to understand what she was saying.

"Tildy treasures certain little bits of clothing. She won't wear them because they're so special, the only memory of her mother that she has."

Her words stabbed at him piercing him with condemnation. Had he done that to them? To all of them? Made them afraid to remember the girl who dashed out and met life head-on, regardless of how much it hurt? Wade bent his head so his face was buried in Clarissa's hair and tried to think through what she'd said.

"I've got pictures and stuff." His nose twitched at her soft lavender fragrance. "In storage. I thought having them around would make them sad, so I packed them away. I—I can't talk about her death. But it was my mistake that caused it."

"I don't believe that, Wade." She lifted her head away and leaned back to peer up at him. "But never mind. Maybe some day you'll tell me about it. For now, focus on the kids. You wanted them to forget because you want to forget the hurt." She nodded. "I know. But they can't forget all of it. They need to remember that she loved them, they need to believe that she would be proud of what they're becoming."

He thought it over. She was right. Kendra *would* be so blown away by her kids' maturity. They'd struggled through so much and yet none of them had ended up as bitter and frustrated as he'd been at their age.

Clarissa's intelligent eyes were studying him again, assessing him. He didn't like it. They saw things he wasn't ready to talk about. He pulled her back into his arms, and held her the way he'd wanted to for days now.

"What made you so smart?" he teased, unable to cover the gruffness that shielded his feelings.

She sniffed, but her eyes clouded over with sadness as she pulled away to glare at him. "Time. A whole lifetime of wanting a family of my own." Her voice was little, scared like a kid's. "I know it sounds dumb, but I always envied the other children their cousins and aunts and uncles. I never had that.''

Her disarming honesty touched him deeply. ''It doesn't sound stupid. It sounds normal. I never was normal, I guess. I only ever wanted to get away from my family. To be free.''

''To do what?'' Her breath brushed warmly past his chin.

Wade shrugged. ''I dunno. To do all the things kids want to do, I guess. Eat what I wanted, when I wanted, sleep all day, sky dive. Anything that I wouldn't have to answer for.'' He laughed at himself bitterly. ''Stupid.''

''It's not stupid. It's perfectly normal. You were sick of being the responsible one, the one to blame. You shouldn't have had to be. Your parents took on that job and then dumped it on you. That was wrong.'' Her voice came softly through the stillness of the evening.

The windows were open, but the evening was as silent as if they alone inhabited the planet. Wade knew he couldn't stay like this much longer. It was asking for trouble. Clarissa got to him like no woman ever had, made him ask himself questions that he didn't have answers for.

She made him wonder if he deserved her, if that soft spot she'd made in his chest would ever grow into something stronger, and what he would do if it did.

He set her gently away with a rueful smile. ''I was wrong earlier.'' He studied her in the faint pink glow of her bedroom lamp. ''Your skin is perfect for those bones. You look lovely.''

She blushed, but didn't look away. "It's all right," she whispered. "I know I'm no Venus."

Almost of its own volition, his hand lifted, one finger tracing the stubborn tilt to her chin, grazing over the porcelain skin. "Venus was untouchable," he muttered, marveling at the softness of her cheek as his rough thumb scraped against the fragility of her smooth forehead.

Clarissa stood there, silent. At one point, when his finger moved to touch her lashes, she closed her eyes, silent and trusting under his touch. In some far-off part of him, Wade knew he shouldn't be touching her. And yet he had to. It connected him to her, somehow. He felt as if he could see her as a child, solemn, dutiful, but never yelling like a banshee as she tore across the unmown grass, or plunged beneath the icy water of a spring river just for the sheer pleasure of feeling it on her skin. He'd done all that and more.

Her voice broke into his memories. "Wade?"

"Uh-huh."

"Could you kiss me? Please?"

It was evident from her tone that she didn't expect him to do it. And he knew why. Clarissa had this idea that she was some kind of plain Jane. That was partly his fault. Somehow he always got the words out wrong when he wanted to tell her she was too fragile to manage all that he'd handed her.

Maybe this was one way to restore her self-confidence.

His brain mocked him. He wanted to kiss her, and it had nothing to do with her self-confidence or his.

"I'm sorry. I shouldn't have put you on the spot."

She tried to step away from him, but he held her fast with one arm while his other hand caught her chin and tipped her face up toward his. Then he bent his head and touched her lips with all the reverence and thankfulness he felt whenever he thought of all she'd done for them.

As his mouth covered hers and found a response, Wade forgot all about thankfulness. For a minute he let himself believe that she really was his wife, that they were happily married and it was his right to kiss her like this.

Right! He didn't have any rights where Clarissa was concerned. Certainly not the right to pretend something he knew wasn't real.

Wade gently pulled back, dropping his hands to his sides so she could step away. "Good night, Clarissa. I'm going to work downstairs for a while."

She never said a word, but her big eyes blinked as if to stem tears as she watched him leave. Wade trod quietly down the stairs, brewed a pot of coffee and took it into the little study.

Life was confusing. Sure he cared about Clarissa. She'd gone out of her way for him and he didn't want to see her hurt because of it. But that didn't mean anything. He'd do the same for anyone.

So, what about those feelings? The ones that made him dream of a future together?

He gulped some coffee and winced as it burned all the way down. That's all it was—a dream. He hurt the people he loved. He always had. They expected stuff from him and he could never fulfill those expectations, no matter how hard he tried.

It was the same with Clarissa, he told himself, as

he pulled forward a pad of paper and the calculator. She would expect him to be that dream husband she'd been waiting for, one who was always there for her, spending time with the family, pandering to her every whim. But he wasn't like that. He needed his space, time to organize his thoughts. He was a private person.

Wade got up to open the window and, as he did, he glanced around the little room. Okay, so she'd let him have his space. Here he was, alone.

So, why did his thoughts keep going to the small, gentle woman upstairs with hair like beaten silver and a heart as big as all outdoors?

Chapter Eight

"I've never gone camping before. What do you do?" Pierce stood at the edge of the table almost a week later, watching as Clarissa lifted one after another of the cookies off the sheet and into a plastic container.

"Well, we'll go swimming, of course. And we'll have campfires each night. If you like, you can sleep on the porch. The cabin is quite comfortable." Mentally she checked off cookies on her list and moved to fill the cooler that stood waiting. "Then of course, there are the fireworks."

"They have Fourth of July fireworks at the lake?" Pierce look amazed. "Can I get my own sparkler?"

"We'll see. Did you pack a bag and put in all the things I told you?" She waited for his nod. "Well?"

"I don't need to take a jacket, Clarissa. It's boiling outside!" He glared at the stove. "In here, too."

"Pierce, it cools off at night. How can you sit around the campfire if you're shivering?"

"But Clarissa—"

"Pierce!" Wade's voice was sharp with reproof. "You will obey Clarissa. Go and get a jacket now."

Pierce glared at his uncle, but he did as he was told, leaving Clarissa alone with Wade in the kitchen while the other children bustled around getting ready for the promised trip.

Clarissa turned away, clamping her lips together to prevent the words from escaping. She wanted this to be a happy time, a time to relax and enjoy each other.

"Wow! There's enough food here for two weeks, even with this mob to devour it." Wade poked a finger into the icing bowl that sat nearby and ran it around the edge. "Keep the cake for me. I love chocolate." He closed his eyes, obviously savoring the dark richness.

"I'm sure you'll get your share." She forced her attention back on the cooler, trying to ignore the shiver of excitement that wiggled up her spine. "I deliberately packed a lot of food because I don't want to have to run to the store. Everything is so expensive in these resort villages."

His hand on her arm stopped her from continuing. "Clarissa, we're not going to starve. You don't have to scrimp all the time."

"Waste not, want not," she muttered, reminding herself of her vow to try to cut corners so he wouldn't have to work so long and so hard.

"I've always hated that saying." He stuck out his tongue at her as if he were Pierce.

"I want to talk to you about something, Wade."

He waggled a finger at her, shaking his head. His

fingers on her arm prevented her from moving away from him. "Uh-uh, you're trying to change the subject. Tell the truth, Clarissa. When was the last time you actually bought something for yourself? I notice the girls have new sandals and there's a box with a dinghy in the front porch that I assume is for the boys. What's your gift?"

"I don't need anything. My clothes wear for years, and I have new sandals that I bought for my vacation in Hawaii." With her eyes, she challenged him to argue. "I did pick up two new shirts for you, though. I can't mend those blue ones anymore. Do you have a partiality for blue? You have six blue shirts."

He shook his head, but his eyes were troubled. "Kendra bought them. It was her favorite color."

"Oh." She didn't know what else to say. The fun and gaiety had drained away.

"What did you want to ask me?"

"What?" She jerked out of her daydream about families at lakes and stared at him. "Pardon?"

He sighed, picked up the pitcher of lemonade and poured himself a glass. "You said you had something to discuss. What is it?" While he waited, he swallowed half the drink. "Well? Am I supposed to guess?"

"No. Uh, sit down, Wade." She tried to think of the right way to approach this.

"Why?" His suspicious glance warned her he was wary. "Is it bad news? Are we overdrawn or something?"

"Of course not. Though we will be if that golf club job isn't soon paid for." She fiddled with a stack of pop cans. "No, it's something else. Something I've been thinking of for a while now."

"Okay." He sat, his eyes darker than usual. "Shoot."

"You know how much trouble I've had with my car? It spends more time in the garage than the mechanics." She let out a squeak of laughter that sounded as false as it felt.

Wade obviously agreed because he frowned at her as if he thought she was sick. "Just say it, Clarissa. You want to stay here, is that it? You don't want to come on the camping trip. Can't say I blame you. It must be driving you nuts having us underfoot all the time."

"No! That isn't it." She took a deep breath and said, "I want to buy a van. A minivan. I've got one all picked out, too."

He blinked. "So that's what he meant?"

"Who?"

"The pastor. He was at the game last night and said something about my life changing for the better. When I asked him what he meant, he said he figured hauling the kids around would be a lot easier for you if you didn't have to worry about reliability. That's all he would say."

"It's his brother's van. They don't want it now that their kids are away from home. It's three years old, has every feature we could possibly want." It came out in a tumbling rush of words and Clarissa stopped, breathless.

"It is a good idea," Wade nodded, sipping his lemonade. "But he'll want his money up front and there's no way I can swing buying a van now. No matter how much he wants.''

She told him the price, steeling herself for the next bombshell. ''You don't have to. I want to buy it myself.''

''No. I'm not going to have my wife going to the bank to take out a loan so we can buy a van.'' A muscle in his jaw flicked as he clenched it, his eyes on the floor. ''I know they wouldn't give me one because I'm self-employed and I haven't got the kind of credit rating they want. But you're not putting your job up as collateral. I won't let you.''

''You won't *let* me, Wade?'' she repeated archly. ''Just now you called me your wife. Well, if that's what I am, then let me be a wife. I have some money put away. It was a gift from my grandmother when she thought I was marrying Harrison. I never touched it because it always brought back some bad memories.''

''Now you want to drive a van around to remind you of him?'' There was bitterness and yes, maybe even envy in his voice.

She laughed, enjoying the very idea of it. ''Hardly! Believe me, I was only too happy to forget him. No, I just meant that there's no reason not to use it now. How can we go to the lake with all this stuff and four kids piled in one compact car, Wade? It doesn't make sense.''

''I'll take the truck,'' he insisted stubbornly.

''Drive two vehicles, spend two tanks of gas? Come on. That's silly.'' She sat down opposite him, prepared to duke it out, if necessary. She had no intention of letting him refuse her this time. ''Why don't you want me to be a part of this family, Wade? Why won't you let me inside that little circle? If I'm your wife, start treating me like one.''

"I haven't stopped you from being part of this family.'' His eyes burned her with their fury.

"Haven't you, Wade?''

She got up and left the room, left the house, too. She couldn't stay there anymore. Not right now. Instead, she walked into the park next door, found a secluded spot in the shade, and poured out her hurt feelings and aching heart to the Father.

Wade watched her go, hands clenched at his sides. Why did she insist on doing this? Burying him further and further in her debt? Who knew how long it would take him to pay her for a van, let alone the other things she'd splurged on with money he knew hadn't come from the checking account he deposited into.

"You hurt her feelings.'' Jared stood behind him. "She was so excited about that van, she thought it was such a good idea. And you spoiled it for her. Why did you do that, Uncle Wade? Why did you hurt her? Clarissa wouldn't do anything to hurt you.''

"You don't understand, Jared.'' Wade bit down his frustration in order to reason with the boy. "I can't afford a van right now.''

"She wasn't asking you to afford anything. She was asking you to accept a gift that she wants to give.'' Jared walked over and flopped into the chair Clarissa had sat in. His face was sad. "She tries so hard to do things for us. Last night I got up to get a drink of water and she was down here making a batch of cinnamon buns because you liked them.''

''She shouldn't go to all that trouble,'' Wade muttered, his voice gruff. ''She wears herself out because of us and I don't want that.''

''But she loves to do it! That's what makes her happy. Yesterday was her day off and she took us shopping at the mall. I didn't really want to go. You know how I hate trying on clothes?'' He waited for Wade's nod. ''But I went anyway because she was so excited about it. She had it all figured out. We got the girls those sandal things, Pierce another pair of pants and your shirts. Then we went to the theater. She said she'd always wanted to go there when it was really hot outside, just to cool off, but she never had anyone to go with.''

Wade refused to let the poignant words get to him. ''A van is a little more expensive than some theater tickets, Jared.''

The boy nodded, his long narrow face thoughtful. ''I know. But it's her money. And this is what she wants. Why do you have anything to say about it?'' he asked, without bothering to mince his words. ''Why is it so wrong to make her happy? She does things for us all the time.''

''Buying that van will make her broke.''

''How do you know? Maybe she'll feel really rich, driving around all over town in it. Maybe she'll feel like a real mother. That's what she wants most.''

Wade stared. ''She wants to be a mother? How do you know this?''

Jared's freckled skin flushed a deep, embarrassing red.

"Well?" Wade didn't relent in his scrutiny.

"I heard her praying one day."

"Jared!" Wade's temper rose like mercury in the desert. "How dare you!"

"I didn't mean to. I was shelving books one day, and she was supposed to be having a coffee break. I went to ask her something but she was praying so I just waited a minute. She was thanking God that He'd given her the chance to have a family, even if it was borrowed. She prayed for all of us, individually. It was kind of nice. Reminded me of Mom." He slapped a hand over his mouth, obviously only just realizing what he'd said.

Wade sighed. So Clarissa had been right there, too. The kids wanted to talk about Kendra but were afraid to around him. Was she right about other things, too? Things like him deliberately shutting her out?

"Your mom prayed for you a lot. She always said you guys were God's gifts to her and could never thank Him enough." Wade swallowed down the hurt and continued. He should have done this months ago. "She had so many plans for you. She used to sit out on the haystack and dream of what you would each be when you were grown up."

Jared's face tightened up, but that didn't stop him from speaking his mind. "Did you love my mother?"

Wade nodded. "I sure did. She was a pain in the butt sometimes, but she was my kid sister. I couldn't help but love her from the first time she flashed those big brown eyes. When she got bigger, I teased her about her lisp." He shook his head, remembering how mean he'd been. "Kendra didn't care what I said, she just had to tag along wherever I went. She'd get mad if I made her stay behind and her lisp would get worse until no one could understand what she was saying. Boy, that girl had a temper!"

"So did Dad." Jared rubbed the back of his hand across his eyes. "I hated it when they were fighting. They tried to keep it down so we didn't hear, but I always listened. It hurt, Uncle Wade."

Wade reached out and clapped a hand on his shoulder. "I know."

"Why did they get married, Uncle Wade? Did they start out in love and then it died, or something? Is that what's gonna happen with you and Clarissa? Do you think she'll get tired of trying to be in our family?"

Wade could have burst out bawling. Or he could have smashed his fist onto the table. Anything to relieve the pent-up emotion that roiled inside at the problems he'd caused with his blind selfishness. But he did neither. Instead he focused on the boy and tried to reassure him.

"Do you think that after waiting all this time for a family, Clarissa is going to just give up? That doesn't sound much like her." He waited for Jared's nod of agreement. "I think Clarissa is going to do everything she can to be the best stand-in mom you guys could have."

"But it isn't going to work if she isn't happy, Uncle Wade." Jared's forehead rippled with worry. "We've got to do things to help her feel like she's part of us, that we want her to stay." He watched Wade anxiously.

Wade sighed. The kid was right. If he expected

Clarissa to be the kind of mother the kids needed, he was going to have to open up to her. The secrets he kept stuffed down inside, that's what was standing between them. He couldn't tell her, couldn't tell anybody, about his part in Kendra's misery, and yet that was at the bottom of all their problems. He was guilty and not worth all her time and attention.

"Uncle Wade?"

"I'll try, kid. I promise I'll really try."

"And you'll go and find her and at least look at the minivan? It's kind of a good idea, Uncle Wade. Her car is pretty cramped, and that van has lots of room. Plus headphones for the ones in back." Jared stopped, obviously wondering if he should have given away this tidbit of information.

Wade burst out laughing. "Well, that clinches it! Headphones are a must." He ruffled the boy's hair, then hugged him close. "Thanks for the pep talk, kiddo."

Jared blushed. "It wasn't really a pep talk. I just wanted to explain. Clarissa's kind of like me. She keeps things inside, where nobody can see them, so that when her feelings get hurt, nobody will know. She doesn't want anybody to think she expects stuff from them."

"You're pretty smart. Know that?" Wade grinned at his perceptive nephew. "For a kid."

"I'm pretty smart, period. But I won't let it go to my head." Jared grinned, high-fived him, then grabbed a cookie and rushed out the back door. "I gotta go check with Evan North about a snorkeling set. See ya!"

"See ya," Wade mumbled, knowing what he had

to do and yet dreading it. "Maybe if I just agree to the van, we won't have to get into the past," he mumbled as he set out for the park. He was almost there before the reality of what he was contemplating hit him. Expose his deepest thoughts to Clarissa's probing honesty? "Why do women always have to dig around in the past?"

"Because men won't." Clarissa voice startled him. She stood at the edge of the trees, hands thrust down into the pockets of her flowing cotton skirt. "What's wrong now?"

"Nothing." He studied her, standing there in her sleeveless white eyelet blouse, her hair tumbling wildly from its topknot. "Do you want to comb your hair before we go check out this van or what?"

Her eyes came alive, flashing and glinting with a joy that shook him to the core. Why did she never smile like that for him?

"You'll let me pay for it?" she demanded, then didn't wait for an answer. "Oh, thank you, Wade. Thank you, thank you, thank you."

She threw herself into his arms, wrapping her hands around his neck as she lifted her feet free of the ground. Wade grabbed her around the waist to keep from being knocked over, and swung her around with a laugh that couldn't be suppressed. After all, that's what Clarissa did, made him laugh when he didn't deserve to.

"If that's what will make you happy, who am I to stand in the way?" he murmured, enjoying the feel of her in his arms, the warm scent of her lavender perfume tickling his nose. "How can I deny you such happiness?"

"You can't!" She giggled with pure delight, pressed tiny kisses all over his face, then pushed away from him to do a little jig in the grass.

"Do you know how long I've wanted to be rid of that horrible car?" she laughed, her hair trailing out behind her in a curtain of waves, the topknot completely destroyed. "Years!"

"Why didn't you, then?" he asked curiously, folding her hand in his as he walked back to the house with her.

"I never had a good enough reason," she told him solemnly. "You see, Gran taught me that one doesn't just do things on the spur of the moment. You need to think things through, plan your action, be sure of your next step, then carry it out, and all that. She was very big on waste not, want not."

"Did you plan this out carefully?" he demanded, holding open the screen door for her. "Are you sure about blowing your money on this van?"

"Positive." She grinned impishly, showing off her beautiful smile.

"Okay then, let's go look at the thing." He handed her the car keys and her purse. "If you're absolutely certain this isn't going to ruin your life?" He thought of the pension fund she could be subsidizing for her future, but repressed the words when she pinched his arm.

"Ruin it? I have the best life I've ever had! Come on, Wade. Turtles move faster than you." She bustled out the door and was in his truck before he had a chance to open the door.

Her happiness was infectious and Wade found himself discussing the van's assets on the way over to the seller's house. He had more qualms about her decision when he watched her write the check on their account, but he stuffed them down. He'd pushed his own way too many times. It was time to sit back and see how this worked out.

Besides, it was her life and she was old enough to decide how she wanted to spend it. He just prayed she'd spend a little more of it with him.

"This was the best idea we've had yet," Clarissa whispered to him on the Fourth of July, her shoulder pressed against his on the rough bench they shared with a host of other campers anxious to see every detail of the fireworks. "Look at them, laughing and giggling like regular kids."

He grimaced. "Well, they're as dirty as the others anyway."

"Oh, don't be such an old poop," she chided, her face inches away from his in the dusky evening. "You've had a good time, too. Admit it, why don't you?"

"I've had a wonderful time," he agreed, studying her face. "Searching the bottom of a frigid lake for a paddle that won't stay attached to the dinghy *you* bought."

"Hey, I got a good deal on it at a yard sale! You can't expect mint condition." She wiggled on the bench. "So there were one or two pieces missing."

"Oar holders are a necessary feature of that dinghy," he muttered, his blood pressure rising as her hauntingly beautiful face glowed in the light from the fireworks. Her eyes were starry bright, like a little kid waiting for Santa. "I also had a wonderful time

trying to put out that forest—er, campfire you built.
We're lucky it rained!''

She blushed adorably, and Wade longed to wrap
his arm around her and hug her close. Which was an
absolutely stupid idea. This was a marriage of convenience, for Pete's sake! She sure didn't want him
fawning over her.

"I didn't realize the boys had put on that lighter
fluid. It's lucky no one was hurt." She perched her
elbows on her knees and stared off into the night.
"Not like the popcorn."

He groaned. "You had to remind me." Wade
opened his palm and grimaced at the two blisters that
lay white and stark against the darkness of his skin.
"Throw that relic out! Nobody pops popcorn over
an open fire anymore. They have hot air poppers or
microwaves, or even skillets."

"I'm an old-fashioned kind of girl." She turned
her head to peer up at him through the gloom. "I
like old stuff like that popper. They remind me of
the past and how much fun somebody else had before
video games and television."

"Yeah, like when the popcorn filled up the basket
and had nowhere to go except by pushing the lid off
and falling into the fire, thereby sending the whole
batch into oblivion." He shook his head, remembering the kernels that had flown out every which way,
pinging anyone within twenty feet, but most especially him. "If it's so much fun, how come you
didn't take that poker-hot thing from me?"

"Ah, poor baby." She lifted his hand, opened his
fingers and placed her lips on each of the burns.
"There, does that make it better?"

Wade's blood pressure hit the danger zone. He shook his head slowly, his eyes riveted to her laughing face. "No, that doesn't help one single bit," he muttered huskily, watching her eyes widen.

She stared at him for a long time. Wade had just decided to go ahead and kiss her when a sonic boom broke the mood and she looked away.

"Oh, look, Wade!" In her excitement she grabbed his injured hand and squeezed it tight.

Not for anything would Wade have pulled away. In fact, with her fingers wrapped around his like that, he barely felt the pain of his burn. Nor did he let her delicate little hand go. It might well be that he was acting juvenile, callow and that he was taking advantage, but he didn't give a fig. For just a few minutes he belonged here beside her, no expectations, no duty, just the two of them enjoying some time together.

While Clarissa watched the fireworks, Wade watched her. She was so cute in her long fluttery flowered skirt and ordinary cotton T-shirt, pink-tipped toes peeking out from her sandals. There was nothing unusual about her, she looked like a zillion other women at this fairground.

And yet, there was something extraordinarily unique about this woman. With just one look from those swirling eyes, she could make him forget about two-by-fours and floor joists. This weekend, he was supposed to be planning a renovation for the widow Saltzburg, his richest client so far and the most challenging job he'd landed.

But all he could do was watch Clarissa teach Pierce to swim, play water polo with her and Jared and provide the sunscreen while the girls tanned. Whenever she looked at the kids, there was love, bright and true, shining in her eyes. A touch, a smile, a softly spoken word. In so many ways Wade could see how much she cared for them.

Why didn't she ever look like that at him? Didn't she want a normal marriage?

Yet still Clarissa treated him as if he were…what? The boss? No, not exactly. The kids' guardian? Yeah, but it was more than that. She treated him as if he were her good friend, almost like a brother.

As Wade studied her pale profile in the light of the rocket bursts, he knew he wanted more than friendship from her. He'd detested that canopy bed of hers for weeks now because it reminded him of her innocence and his lack of it.

But sleeping at the cabin was infinitely worse. Every night she crawled into her own sleeping bag, leaving him wishing he had the right to hold her close, to kiss her more than a peck on the cheek.

It was ridiculous, really. He was the one who wanted to be free, unencumbered, a loner. He'd always wanted to go his own way, forge his own path. Yet now, he craved Clarissa's touch, her gentle smile, her soft encouraging words.

Worst of all, he had no right to think about a future, a real marriage with Clarissa. Not until he told her the truth. Then she'd probably decide that she didn't want a deserter in her life and it would serve him right.

"Oh, wasn't that a beauty?" She dropped her head on his shoulder, content to watch the waterfall of cascading fireworks as they died away into the last embers.

Wade slipped his arm around her waist and held her, a swell of something bursting inside as he supported her head, his fingers tangling in the silken stream of hair that flowed down her back. Why couldn't he just tell her that he wanted more from this relationship? That he wanted to get rid of the wall he'd kept up and finally share a part of himself with someone else, someone who really mattered, to form a bond that would last no matter what. How could he want this closeness—crave it? Would she ever agree to it?

As the crowds in the stands stood and began to leave, he came back to reality with a thud.

No, Wade shook his head mentally. It would never work out. She was a homebody, a nester. He was a rolling stone.

But just for a moment Wade let himself imagine what it could have been like. If only he didn't always have to be the responsible one.

Chapter Nine

"What a dreary job on such a lovely day."

Two weeks later Clarissa dusted off the library's encyclopedias for the third time, her mind busy with thoughts of the lake. It had been a wonderful three-day vacation, everything she'd hoped for. They'd laughed and giggled and had fun. Even Wade had forgotten that taciturn manner and had unbent enough to join in the water fight.

She blushed remembering their walks in the woods after the kids had gone to bed when he'd kissed her as if she were a rare and precious object, the times around the fire when his hand had caught hers and held it fast, the way he sneaked up behind her and kissed her on the neck when nobody was looking.

Wade had changed. She felt that he'd loosened up a little, though there was nothing specific in his demeanor that she could put her finger on. He whistled a lot these past few weeks and teased the kids into a good mood when their plans were rained out. He hadn't said even a word of protest when she bought a microwave with the money that was left from the van.

He was also more affectionate. Which was nice, but Clarissa wanted more than affection. She didn't want to go to sleep alone. Maybe that's why she liked mornings so much. Wade wasn't a morning person. The alarm clock buzzed for a long time before it penetrated his blurry brain.

For Clarissa it was a golden opportunity to lie there and watch him sleep. Sometimes she reached out and touched his hair. It was as glossy and black as a raven's wing and lately had grown quite long. She never mentioned it, though. She liked it that way, liked to see its blue-blackness caught in a morning sunbeam.

Some mornings she leaned over and kissed his cheek, just the way she would if they were really husband and wife. Sometimes she just stared at him and begged God to make him love her.

But the second the alarm issued its annoying beep, she whipped into the bathroom to have her shower so she wouldn't hold him up. By the time he came down, breakfast was ready, she was neat and tidy and the house had been straightened. He might never love her, but Clarissa was determined that he would never find her a burden, either. She would do her part no matter what.

"Clarissa, what is wrong with you? I've asked three times for that book on zinnias." Mrs. Rothschild tapped her cane on the floor abruptly. "I don't hold with daydreaming, you know. Focus on the present. It gets more things done."

"Yes, Mrs. Rothschild." Clarissa moved to behind the counter, found and stamped the book and handed it to her. "I hope you enjoy it. It's not due for a month, so take your time."

"Won't need it that long. I read very fast."

Mrs. Rothschild disapproved of taking her time over anything, and Clarissa knew it from the other woman's fraternization with her grandmother years ago.

Mrs. Retter peered over the desk, her eyes darting here and there through her tiny round spectacles. "My turn, dear. My book on asparagus?"

"I've saved it for you. Right here. It looks very interesting." Clarissa handed it over, then turned away from the two ladies who were busy discussing an upcoming rummage sale. "Jared, could you run these letters to the post office? Take Pierce with you and stop for an ice cream on the way back. That's an order."

"Yes, ma'am!" Jared saluted smartly, grinned as he pocketed the letters, then hurried off to find his brother. Clarissa turned back to her work with a smile.

"She says the work was inferior."

The voice was Mrs. Rothschild's. She must be standing behind the magazine stacks, for Clarissa couldn't see her. She shrugged, ignoring the whispered discussion until Wade's name pricked her ears.

"It's no wonder, is it now? The man is working far too many hours. How can he do a good job when he rushes from one job to another?"

Mrs. Retter tut-tutted. "I don't think that's what she said, dear. I think she was implying that he used poor material. That's why she fell. You know how it is nowadays. Knotty this and second grade that.''

Mrs. Rothschild sniffed in a way Clarissa knew only too well.

"If you hire that sort, you must expect that they take shortcuts. If you talk to Hilda again, tell her I shall stop by tomorrow, whether she likes it or not. At eighty-six, she can't afford to keep playing this hermit's game. She should be in a nursing home.''

"She hates the home. Says it takes away her independence. Why, do you know she eats breakfast at eleven-thirty in the morning? I might try that.''

The whispering got fainter and fainter as the two moved toward the door, then through it. Clarissa frowned. Hilda had to be the widow Saltzburg, especially since they'd called her a hermit. The widow seldom, if ever, came to town. That's why Clarissa often had to send someone up to the mansion with her order of books.

Wade's next job was there, wasn't it? Clarissa remembered how happy he'd been to land the contract. She'd tried to warn him about the grumpy, perfectionistic harridan, but he'd brushed off her concern.

"I've built my reputation around here on good, solid work. She can't argue with that, now can she?''

"It was probably nothing,'' she told herself. "Quit worrying and think about what you're going to make for dinner.''

By the time she got home, Tildy had arrived and scrubbed down the kitchen floor, so Clarissa decided to take a shower while she waited for it to dry.

Dressed once more in a tank top and shorts, she felt much cooler.

"Hi, guys!" The kids, three of them anyway, sat grouped around the table. "What do you want to eat tonight?"

"Ice water," Lacey muttered, swiping her hand across her head.

"Anything that doesn't take an oven." That was Tildy, fanning herself with the phone book.

Clarissa was about to open the fridge when the phone rang. "I'll get it. Hello?"

A tirade of anger poured over the lines in the aggrieved tones of one widow Saltzburg. "That young man should be barred from going into other people's homes and creating havoc. It's his fault I've hurt myself. He's careless. Yes, and sloppy, too. Imagine using such poor quality materials that I fell through them."

Clarissa started to speak, but it was quite clear that the widow had not finished. She ranted and raved for a good five minutes more.

"Those kind of people should be forced to go to school and learn the proper way to do things. How could you marry that kind of man, my dear? You're not a stupid girl, not since you got rid of that silly Harrison, anyway." The widow cackled nastily. "He was a taker. And I fear this one is the same. He's no good, you know. Wasn't raised right. He's certainly not our kind."

Clarissa unclenched her fingers one by one until she held the phone loosely in her hand. She took a deep breath and cut right through the spurious remarks about Wade's character.

"Mrs. Saltzburg, I will thank you to stop spouting such defamatory remarks about the man I've married. I assure you that I know him quite well, and he is by no means unskilled or untrained. In fact, his work is in demand all over town. He works night and day, and I happen to know that he put several other people on hold because you demanded that he do your work right away!" She stopped for a breath.

"Well, miss, perhaps he did." The old lady harrumphed in disgust. "That doesn't change the facts. He's ruined my place, just simply ruined it. That man is bad news, young lady."

Clarissa sniffed. She hadn't been called that since she was ten, but it no longer intimidated her.

"I wasn't finished speaking, Mrs. Saltzburg," she said quietly. "'That man' voluntarily took over the care and feeding of his four nieces and nephews so that they would have a good stable home, food on the table and a built-in support system. He didn't have to, but he did it to prevent their family being broken up."

"Probably to get at their money." The snide comment whispered over the line.

Clarissa saw red. "Oh, yes, of course, that's the reason. That's why we live in such luxury. Listen to me, Mrs. Saltzburg." Clarissa ignored the noise behind her, figuring the kids were up to something. That would have to wait. But this maligning of Wade's work and his character wouldn't.

"My husband leaves for work in the morning before any of the children are up. He works the entire day, often not returning home until long after they've gone to bed. He missed seeing them in the school play, misses chatting with them, misses many of their special moments, just so he can make sure they have what they need. And he does this, not because he's trying to steal from them, but because he wants to make sure they never have to go without, as he did.''

''All very praiseworthy, I'm sure.'' The snideness again came through loud and clear.

Clarissa ignored that. ''Yes, it is praiseworthy. Even more so is the fact that, despite your changing the plans several times since he bid on your project, Wade has never had one miserable word to say about you, or about anyone else in this town. For that matter, he doesn't complain at all. He just goes about doing the best work he can. Which in your case, I might add, is being done for far less than anyone else would charge.''

''It's faulty work,'' the querulous old woman insisted. ''I don't pay for faulty work.''

''Is it really?'' Clarissa squeezed her eyes shut and counted to ten, praying for heavenly direction. ''Well then, Mrs. Saltzburg, I'll have Wade and his lawyer out there first thing tomorrow morning. They'll take pictures, assess the problem. If the work is without fault, as I know it will be, I'm afraid Wade will be advised to seek some compensation. He won't want to, of course. But his lawyer will insist that he not allow your spurious remarks about his character or his work.'' She waited a moment, then dropped the bombshell. ''I'm afraid all work on your house will have to cease until this is sorted out.''

Wade stood where he was, directly behind Clarissa, his mouth cracking into a smile as he heard the widow squawking something into the receiver. He couldn't believe his ears. Prim, perfect, calm and quiet Clarissa had defended *him*. And so staunchly, too. He couldn't help smiling at the words she'd used. First-class, top-notch, superior. She liked his work!

"Perhaps you didn't mean to suggest such a thing, but that *is* what I heard, Mrs. Saltzburg. Talk like that is dangerous, not to mention hurtful."

Wade couldn't hear what the cranky widow was saying, so he reached around Clarissa and stabbed the speaker phone button. His wife whirled around, eyes wide with surprise. He caught her in his arms, his finger on her lips to stop her from interrupting the apology that flowed from the telephone.

"I'm sure I never meant to imply anything negative about the man, Clarissa. It's just that one hears talk and I did want to warn you about what was being said."

"You don't need to warn me about Wade Featherhawk, Mrs. Saltzburg. I know everything I need to know about him." Clarissa held his eyes with her steady gaze, her voice firm and unrelenting. "There's nothing you or anyone else could say that would alter my opinion of him."

"Yes, of course. And you would know him best, dear. Please accept my humblest apologies. I certainly didn't mean to upset anyone. There's no need at all for lawyers or any of that nonsense. Now that I think about it, I'm sure I stumbled because of that carpet runner. Beacock is always leaving it too loose." They heard her bellow something then she came back on the line.

"There's no need at all to bother the man with my little fall, dear. I'll expect him tomorrow, as usual. I'm anxious to see how he finishes the summer house."

She prattled on for a few minutes more, alternately apologizing and seeking reassurance that Wade wouldn't know of her call. She hadn't meant a word of it, she insisted.

"Tell her goodbye," Wade whispered in her ear.

"I'm sorry, Mrs. Saltzburg, but I have to get dinner for the children. Goodbye." She hung up the phone and clicked the speaker button off, trying to ease out of his embrace as she did.

Wade knew she was thinking of the kids, but he'd shooed them all out as soon as he figured out who was calling and why. Now he kept his hands firmly in place on her waist and tipped up her chin with one finger.

"She apologized. I can't believe it! After all the miserable things she's said today, I was ready to quit." He shook his head in disbelief. "What on earth did you say to change her mind?"

Clarissa's face grew pink. Her eyes flew away from his curious stare, her hands fiddled with the button on his shirt. "I just told her the truth."

"You defended me. I heard it—part of it, anyway." He couldn't quite believe it even now. No one had ever defended him before. Clarissa had said she knew everything she needed to know about him and yet, Wade knew she didn't. He'd kept the worst of his past a deep, dark secret. "Why did you do it, Clarissa? I could have stood up for myself."

"I know. You don't need me to stand up for you.

You don't *need* my help or my concern." She tried to swallow the wobble in her voice. "But that's what I do, Wade. I defend people I care about."

She was furious, he could see it in her face so he held his tongue and let her vent.

"She said horrible things, and hinted even worse. I wasn't going to let her get away with that." Her whole body was rigid with anger. "No way."

"But why?" He kept at it, trying to figure it out. Why wouldn't she let the widow get away with it? "What does it matter to you?"

Clarissa glared at him so fiercely, he expected to see steam come shooting out of her ears.

"What does it matter to me? Let me tell you, Wade Featherhawk, I have backbone, and I won't stand for lies. I don't let anyone malign the people I love, especially when they've done nothing wrong. That's why it matters, Wade Featherhawk. Just because your heritage isn't the same as hers is no reason for her nasty little innuendos that hint at some kind of character flaw. I wasn't going to let her get away with that."

For a moment Clarissa looked smugly satisfied with her defense. Then she clapped a hand over her mouth, her eyes riveted on him. "Oh."

"Yes, oh." He grinned, refusing to set her free, though she wiggled like an eel. "You love me, Clarissa?"

She glared at him, then to his utter amazement, strong, defiant Clarissa, champion defender, burst into tears. "Oh, why did you have to come in? Why couldn't you have waited?" She sobbed the words out, her fingernails tapping on his chest in reproof.

Wade took that dainty little hand in his and held on for dear life. He couldn't believe it. She loved him!

"I'm sorry! I didn't mean to tell you. I was trying to keep it a secret."

Wade tenderly mopped her face. "It's all right, Clara," he murmured, snuggling her head into his neck. "It's okay. It was a wonderful thing you did for me. I can't tell you what it felt like to come in and hear you defending me. It was—a new experience."

"Nobody defended you before?" she gasped, her sobs still near the surface. She pulled back to peer at him through the tumble of her hair.

He puffed out a harsh laugh as he brushed the glossy curtain behind her ears. "Usually the opposite. Most of the time, what they said was true." He stared into her dear face and marveled at how easily she'd wound herself into their lives. "I tried to live up to their expectations and ended up doing some pretty awful things, Clara. Nasty things. When I couldn't face up to them, I ran away." He cracked a smile. "But there wasn't anywhere to run and the cops always brought me back home to face the music." He fell into thoughts of those sad days.

"Wade?"

"Yeah?" He stared at her, startled by the compassion he could hear in her quiet voice.

"If you need to get away, be by yourself for a while, I can handle things here. You don't have to stick with us all the time. Why don't you go golfing or something?"

He wanted to cry. It was a ridiculous thing for a

grown man to admit, but the sweet tenderness of her words made his eyes ache with unshed tears. She gave so much, poured herself out for them. And asked nothing in return. Instead she offered even more.

He leaned forward until his forehead was touching hers. "I don't want to go away, Clara," he murmured.

"What do you want to do?" she whispered, a frown wrinkling a furrow of barely tanned skin between her eyebrows.

"This." He dipped his mouth down and covered hers, telling her without words how grateful he was for her concern, her care, her love. At first he hadn't wanted it. Now, he didn't know what to do with it, but he was grateful for it all the same.

Through a fog of enchantment that kissing Clarissa engendered, Wade heard a discreet cough. He frowned, finished kissing Clarissa the way he'd wanted to for weeks now, and turned his head to chew out the interloper.

Four sets of eyes stared at the spectacle of the two of them entwined in each other's arms. Four mouths grinned in smug satisfaction. Only one shocked voice demanded an answer.

"Do you *like* all that mushy stuff, Clarissa?" Pierce apparently couldn't believe such a thing.

Wade took pity on Clarissa and set her free, but not before he hugged her once more. "Thank you," he whispered for her ears alone. "I'm going to have a shower. Please don't turn the water on."

She nodded, but Wade wasn't sure she heard a word. He did hear Tildy ask to get a pizza and go to the park. As he showered, he couldn't help thinking it was a very good idea. This house was far too hot. He supposed he'd have to think about central air for the old barn.

Wade had to admit, he was getting fond of the place, even thought of it as home. That should have bothered him, but it didn't. And Wade had no intention of asking himself why.

It was late by the time they got back from the park. Clarissa straightened up the kitchen while the kids, tired from their impromptu game of volleyball and mad dashes through the sprinklers, tumbled up the stairs and through the shower with scarcely a word of protest.

She avoided Wade as best she could by scurrying through the house to open all the windows and check screens, hoping that the night breeze would cool the place off. By the time she'd finished, the kids were ready to be kissed. Then she took her glass of iced tea, her Bible and hurried out to the veranda, hoping God would send some clear directions on where she should go next.

She was well into Corinthians by the time Wade came out, but the answers still eluded her.

"Why don't you read it out loud? I like to listen to you reading. Your voice is very expressive." He flopped down in the big wicker armchair, his fingers snagging her glass for a quick swallow. "Go ahead. I'm listening."

Clarissa glanced down and gulped. The "love" chapter? She was supposed to read that out loud to him? *All right, God.* She took a breath, then plunged in, reciting I Corinthians as best she could with her eyes closed.

"'If I speak with the tongues of men and of angels, but do not have love, I'm like a noisy gong or a clanging cymbal. If I have all faith, so as to remove mountains, but do not have love, I am nothing. And if I give all my possessions to feed the poor, but do not have love, it profits me nothing.'" She opened her eyes.

"Interesting, isn't it? He seems to be saying that nothing matters much without love." Wade fiddled with his glass. "Finish it, please."

Clarissa took a deep breath and continued.

"'Love is patient, love is kind, and is not jealous; love does not brag; it is not provoked, does not rejoice in unrighteousness, but rejoices with truth. Love bears all things, believes all things, hopes all things, endures all things. Love never fails.'"

"'Love never fails,'" he quoted in a soft whisper.

The night sounds echoed in the background. Crickets nattered away in a constant rhythm, the wind breathed its way through a screen that kept out the high-pitched whine of mosquitoes itching to snack on humans. In the garden, the sprinkler clicked a pattern over, around and back again.

Wade heard it all through the questions that rose in his mind. "Love believes all things." He'd never believed in Clarissa, not even when she married him. He'd always assumed she had some secret agenda of her own, something she wanted from him. And he'd always assumed that he didn't have it in him to give it to her.

But now Wade wondered about that. Why was he

so positive that both he and the kids could depend on Clarissa? What made her any different from the women who'd hounded him in the past? Why was it so easy to go to work and let her handle their problems? It wasn't just that he didn't want to deal with them. He did, but she did a far better job with less fuss and faster results than he'd ever managed. Why did she do that?

The answer lingered deep inside and it took a minute to hear his brain answer. What Clarissa did, she did because she loved them. She was independent enough to stand on her own two feet. She had it all together, she wasn't always searching for something. She didn't *need* him, but he sure needed her.

Oh, sure, she claimed she was in love with him, but if he disappeared today, she'd manage just fine. He could count on her to see things through. Then why did he want to be an integral part of her life, to be the person she depended on, ran to for answers, talked things over with? He wasn't a family man, he'd told her that. Did he want to change now?

Wade studied her as she sat there, head bowed as she perused the words on that fragile onionskin paper. Had she been in love with him before he'd suggested marriage? Had he trampled on her delicate feelings, hurt her with his blunt refusal to do anything but take from her? No responsibilities, he'd told her. No strings.

His face burned as he thought over the words. "Love bears all things, believes all things, hopes all things, endures all things," she'd read. Surely that was a picture of the woman sitting across from him, silently studying her big black Bible. Whatever else she was, Clarissa Cartwright was a gift from God. She didn't play games, didn't try to hide anything. Her clear trusting face gave away her thoughts. With a certainty, Wade knew he could depend on her, count on her to give him a chance.

Why me, he wondered. Why send her my way? I've done nothing but hurt her.

Pictures from their short past tumbled through his brain. Clarissa, lips pinched tight as she forced herself to unhook the fish she'd caught. Clarissa, skirt billowing out behind her as she raced him around the lake. Her head a silver halo in the clear moonlight as she'd sung about moonlight and roses when she thought she was alone. Clarissa, cheeks burning with embarrassment as she insisted that she defended him because she loved him.

He didn't deserve anything she'd given him. He'd taken it all like a greedy kid, without a thought to what she wanted or felt or needed. It had even taken Jared's insight to make him see how much she wanted to buy that van.

He watched as she closed her Bible, got to her feet and wished him good-night. He answered automatically, staring as she left the porch. She moved with a light-footed grace that intrigued him. Why did she always tiptoe around, as if she were afraid she'd disturb him?

She had a skirt on again and it swirled and swayed around her ankles, drawing his attention to her elegant bare feet, slim, pink-tipped toes. Clarissa made no attempt to draw attention to herself and yet, he couldn't stop watching her, couldn't stop his brain from noticing when she bit her lip in concentration, pushed her hands behind her back as if they were in the way, paused before she spoke, giving him time to say what was on his mind.

The clawing in his midsection crawled to his brain. Why did she care? This love she claimed to have— it was an enigma that he wanted to understand. He craved it, desperately wanted to bask in the love she felt for him, to let it flow over and around him, to let it wash away the hard bitter places, ease the hurting that the widow's ugly accusations had resurrected. Was that so wrong?

With a sigh, Wade got up from his chair, locked the house up and climbed the stairs praying for help to understand these strange new feelings that whirled inside like a maelstrom that would not be silent. He coveted the freedom to tell her things, things he'd never told anyone before. He yearned to share a piece of his heart with her, let her see the misery he carried inside. Maybe she could help him get rid of it, cleanse him of this awful guilt for so many failures.

He pushed open their bedroom door, thinking she'd be asleep. The sight of his wife wrapped in what he privately thought of as her rosebud robe, and seated before her little vanity had him rooted to the spot, mesmerized by her long pianist's fingers as they combed through the braids, loosening the strands. When she reached for the brush, he moved forward wordlessly, sliding it from her hands to sweep it through the silver-gilt threads, carefully smoothing them into a cloak of gossamer moonlight.

"Clarissa," he murmured, his fingers lacing through the silken cascade. "I want to make this marriage work."

She sat where she was, head bowed, a dainty figure in a wash of white cotton moonlight. "So do I," she whispered.

"But I don't know how. I look at you and I can't understand why you would love me. There's nothing I could ever do to deserve someone like you. There's no plausible reason why you should care about a guy like me." He kept up the rhythmic strokes, puzzling it out without success. "I'm not the guy you need. I hurt people who care about me, Clarissa. I don't want to, but I always end up hurting them, disappointing them."

In one graceful motion she slipped to her feet and stood in front of him, her hair a glowing static halo cloud around her calm, smiling face.

"I love you, Wade. You can't deserve it, or make me not feel it. You can't change it. All you can do is accept it." Her fingers cupped his cheek, her eyes soft and welcoming as his hands slid to her tiny waist. "I don't expect anything from you. I don't want you to say or do anything. I just want to be your wife."

She stood on her tiptoes, pink toenails softly glowing in the light as they scrunched into the carpet. Wade tipped his head up and watched her mouth move to within millimeters of his.

"Is that okay with you?"

No matter how much he tried, Wade couldn't deny himself this wonderful gift. He felt guilty accepting it, he wanted to explain things, tell her how bad it was inside him where nobody saw, explain that this was all too new—that he didn't know what to do with love like hers.

But maybe that could come later. Right now, it was getting awfully difficult to resist those full pink lips.

"Very okay," he murmured, drawing her close.

Her hands slid around his neck, her fingers tangling in the length of hair that still needed cutting. "Me, too," she whispered before her mouth touched his sweetly.

He kissed her back, then drew away to search her eyes. "You're sure?" His heart dropped when she moved away.

Clarissa pushed the door closed, then laced her fingers in his. "Positive."

A long time later, Wade touched the silver swath of hair that lay against her flushed cheek. She was beautiful inside and out, like the fairy princess his mother had read of so long ago. As she sighed and shifted in her dreams, one blue-veined hand moved to cover his heart. Having Clarissa as his for-real wife was the most wondrous thing imaginable.

Wade reached out to take her hand, to kiss her awake and tell her how much he cared for her. But he stopped midreach, thought again, let his hand fall away. After all, what could he say?

That he wasn't worthy of her love? She already knew that. That he wanted to love her **but** was afraid that once he said the words, she'd end up depending on him for things he couldn't give? That he was scared spitless at the thought of living his life without the rigid control he'd always had over his emotions? A control he knew he would willingly relinquish if ever she asked. That he'd never wanted to be a husband, to be responsible for someone else's happiness?

No, he couldn't do it.

"It doesn't mean I don't care about you, Clarissa," he whispered. The words sounded hollow, empty. And Wade knew such a paltry admission wasn't enough. In fact, compared to her heartfelt gift of trust in a man she knew so little about, it was woefully inadequate.

But for now, it would have to do, because Wade had no intention of telling her how unworthy he was to have anyone love him. He wasn't going to explain that caring about him meant you got hurt. He was just going to make sure that this woman didn't suffer for his faults.

"Love never fails."

They'd just have to wait and see how true that was.

Chapter Ten

Monday, August 24, rolled around, two weeks into the heat wave of the century that threatened to scorch everything in Waseka and the surrounding area.

Clarissa huffed a sigh of relief as she waved a tearful goodbye at the children who waved frantically from the bus now leaving the church parking lot. Off to camp for the last week of summer before school started! Maybe now she could get done some of those jobs around the house that had waited far too long. Working would numb the ache around her heart. She hoped. She loved Wade. She was his wife. Would he never say the words she wanted to hear? Was she fooling herself?

"I missed them, I guess?" Wade took her hand, helped her up over the curb and opened the van door. "I tried to get here in time, but I had a flat. Sorry, Clarissa. I didn't mean to make you handle this all alone."

She climbed into her seat, and wiped a hand across

her forehead. "It doesn't matter. They were so excited, I doubt they noticed I was here. What are you doing today?"

"Nothing! You scheduled those jobs so far apart that I'm free as a lark until the Martins get back from vacation next week. I might even take today off." He grinned like a little boy who'd skipped school. "Wanna help me play hookey?"

She'd specifically taken this week of holidays so she could get caught up on her housework. But when would she next get a chance to spend some free time with her husband, a man she was only now just beginning to really understand? At least, she thought she did.

Clarissa made up her mind in an instant. "Sure. What did you have in mind?"

He grinned, then winked, a devilish glint in those mischievous dark eyes. "Meet you at home."

For the first time in ages, Clarissa didn't consider her food budget. She stopped at the grocery store and stocked up on deli meats, rolls, salads, some ice cream, a dozen lemons and a basket of fresh strawberries.

Those strawberries made her blush. She'd seen movies where the hero had dipped one in chocolate and fed it to the heroine, then kissed her hand, her arm, her neck...well, kissed her!

She wasn't expecting Wade to do that, of course. He didn't need strawberries or anything else to be romantic, or to make her heart thud so hard it hurt. It was just that she craved a melding of their spirits....

Clarissa forced the thought away and wheeled her

cart into the nearest checkout. God is in control, she reminded herself. He wouldn't forsake them. Somehow, it would all work out.

"I'm home," she called, lugging the bag through the front door as the heat dragged at her. Wade was standing in the kitchen, an odd look on his face. He moved forward to take the bag from her, his eyes roiling with some dark emotion. "I stopped to get some— Oh, hi, Rita."

She swallowed her disappointment at seeing the social worker lounging at the kitchen table, chewing on one of the brownies Tildy had insisted on mixing last night.

"I wouldn't eat too many of those, if I were you," Clarissa warned, unpacking everything and storing them in the fridge.

"They do have an odd taste," Rita agreed, sampling another. "But the icing is delicious."

"She tripled the baking powder, hoping to get them to rise. It has a rather, um, odd effect." Clarissa shrugged as Rita helped herself to a third bar. "Or maybe it's just me," she murmured, winking at Wade.

"Some people do have weak stomachs," the other woman agreed. "I was just telling your hubby here that in adoption cases, I like to get the messy stuff dealt with out front, before it causes problems." Her beady eyes fixed on him with a stern look. "You might have told me about your past."

"I didn't realize it was important." Wade shrugged, then leaned against the cupboard, a coffee cup in one hand.

But Clarissa wasn't fooled. He was anything but relaxed.

"Running away from your home, willful destruction, terrorizing the neighbors—that's not important?" Rita wiped her fingers on a napkin and shook her head.

He shook his head, his eyes averted from Clarissa's. "No, it isn't. It was over a long time ago. I was twelve."

"It doesn't exactly qualify you for parent of the year, though. All of this stuff came up in the background check, Mr. Featherhawk."

Clarissa wanted to ask about this "stuff" that Wade never spoke of, but she held her tongue. If God was in control, it was time to let Him handle things.

"How can my childhood interfere with my caring for and adopting my nieces and nephews?" Wade's face darkened, anger evident in the clenched jaw and ticking muscle at the side of his neck.

"It's not just your childhood. You were practically an adult when you stole your uncle's car and ran away from home. You left your sister at home, alone, with no one to watch out for her. Your mother had no idea where you'd gone. It was only sheer chance that the highway patrol officer noticed the trail off into the woods and followed it."

"Kendra wasn't a baby. Besides, I had to get away, to think about my life. It was getting pretty hot at home and I needed a cooling-off time." Wade's low voice oozed with bitterness.

"Children who feel uncomfortable in their home situations often do need a cooling-off period, Rita. That's not a bad thing for a boy to recognize." Clarissa felt compelled to point that out as she watched the misery of the past creep across Wade's glowering face. "It doesn't mean he isn't a good father."

"Sometimes it does." Rita's scrutiny was unrelenting. "Sometimes the past gives us a clue to what the future holds." She straightened, her voice growing harsher as her eyes riveted on Wade.

"I have a responsibility to make sure these kids will not be abandoned just because the going gets rough. Four kids create a lot of heat, Wade. You can't opt to take off and 'think things over,' even if Clarissa is here and the kids are getting older. You've got to commit to a lifetime of being there, of fulfilling their needs first, before your own. I'm concerned that your commitment is going to dwindle down to the point that regret for what you've sacrificed takes its toll on this entire family."

Wade's cup hit the counter with a force that shattered it. He ignored the pieces, his face twisted with anger and something else, something Clarissa could see glinting at the back of his tortured eyes.

"Look, I've said I'll do it, and I will. I know how important this is, Miss Rotheby. I know exactly how much those kids have lost." He stopped, obviously changing what he was about to say. "I give you my vow that I will not leave them, I will not run away from my promise to my sister. I owe her that much."

Clarissa stood, moved over to stand beside Wade, her hand stroking his arm. "We both will, Rita. The kids are doing very well. They've settled in here, Wade is working day and night. We're managing. It's not easy, but we will get through. I promise you that."

Rita glanced from one to the other of them, her eyes speculative. "I'm not worried about you, Clarissa. You've always been bedrock solid, dependable as the sun. It's his predilection for avoiding obligations in the past that has me worried."

"Well, don't be afraid any longer, Miss Rotheby." Wade jerked his arm away from Clarissa, his face dark with fury. "Believe me, I've finished running away. I'm well aware of how my hurry to avoid my duty led to my sister's death. I also know that there is nothing I can do to atone for that, except to look after her children for as long as they need me."

Wade leaned over, brushed a caressing hand through Clarissa's hair, then let it drop away as he straightened. "I'm going out for a while," he told her, his lids hiding the turmoil in his eyes. "I won't be long."

"I'll be here," she promised, ignoring Rita's interested stare. "I'll be right here."

He nodded, his lips pinched tight. "I know. Good old conscientious Clarissa. Backbone of the community."

Clarissa backed away, hurt by the tone in his voice. He closed his eyes and shook his head, raking his fingers through the black length in a gesture that signaled his hurting heart.

"I'm sorry, Clarissa. I didn't mean that the way it sounded. I'm sorry for everything." He left without a backward glance, the screen door slamming shut behind him.

"He's a powder keg, just waiting to blow." Rita dug in her copious bag for a pad and pencil.

Clarissa reached out and touched her fingers, willing her to listen.

"No, Rita. He's worn out and grieving and doing his best to be strong and invincible. Every time he looks at the kids, I think he sees Kendra. He's in a lot of pain."

Rita nodded thoughtfully. "And some of it has to do with his sister's death," she muttered. "I'm a little concerned about that. What did he mean by 'avoiding his duty'?" She peered up at Clarissa, waiting for an answer.

But Clarissa couldn't answer, because he hadn't told her, hadn't explained the one detail of his past that still held the power to tear him apart. He didn't trust her enough.

"You'll have to ask Wade," she murmured, sadness creeping through her tired body. "I can't answer for him. But I will assure you of this. He isn't going to run out on me or them. He's committed to this marriage. He's committed to this family."

Rita huffed to her feet. "If anybody can bring him around, Clarissa, you can. You're strong enough for the both of you." She said thank you for the brownies, picked up her bulging briefcase and waddled out the door.

Tears welled in Clarissa's eyes. "I'm not strong at all," she muttered. "I'm just too afraid to ask him outright what happened in the past. I'm afraid, Lord."

She spent a few moments asking for heavenly direction, then, since Wade hadn't returned, decided to stick to the original plan and get to work on the basement. The youth group needed a cool place to meet for their Bible study. If she could fix up an area down there, it would be perfect.

The boxes from Wade and the children's move were stacked helter-skelter all over, some with their contents tumbling out.

"Jared, I might have known you'd dump your schoolbooks down here." She pushed the stack of looseleaf into an empty box and set it aside for a fire she'd have later. There were winter clothes, photo albums, pots, pans, curtains and a host of other things that she sorted into two piles, give-away and storage.

As she carted the last of the storage cartons to a place under the stairway, Clarissa stumbled over a small brown box that must have fallen out of one of the others. She flipped it open, wondering which stack it belonged in.

The name of a prominent university leapt out at her from a letter addressed to Wade. She recognized the envelope as one that had arrived only last week. Her eyes scanned the words, as the ache inside grew.

"He wanted to go to school," she whispered, recognizing the date for classes to begin as only weeks away. "An architect. He was going to train as an architect."

She lifted the letter and read about the funding in place for mature students. Because his preliminary marks were so high and his renderings so technically correct, one of the professors had recommended a very generous tuition scholarship.

"This is a one-time only offer," the letter stated. "We reserve the right to withdraw it if you do not appear on September 15."

He gave it up. He gave it all up to raise Kendra's

kids. The knowledge caused a surge of tenderness to rise inside Clarissa. How long had it taken to acquire the credits necessary for entrance to the faculty? She remembered him once telling the kids that he'd never finished his senior year.

As her fingers loosed on the box, it tumbled to the floor and papers scattered everywhere. Columns, turrets, gable roofs and transom windows, precise in every perspective, lay scattered across the floor.

"Clarissa?" Wade's voice broke through her study of the sketches.

"I'm down here," she replied, forcibly restraining herself from hiding the evidence of her meddling.

He got halfway down before his eyes flew to the white papers littering the cement. He didn't say a word, merely looked at her.

"I was straightening up these boxes," she whispered. "You know, so the youth group could meet here. These fell out."

He stalked down the rest of the stairs and toward her, stopping along the way to pick up his drawings.

"I didn't mean to pry, Wade. Truly, I didn't."

He ignored her words. "Doesn't matter. I should have thrown them away. It's past."

The utter void of any expression of feeling in those words made her want to weep.

"It doesn't have to be," she murmured, resting one hand on his arm. "You could still attend classes. I could get a job...."

Her voice trailed away as he turned on her, his lips stretched in a mocking grin. "Oh, sure. You could find a job that would support six people while I whiled away the hours at school? Come on, Clarissa. Be realistic. It isn't going to happen.''

"Perhaps if we—"

"Just let it die! It was a stupid idea. I'd probably make a lousy architect, anyhow. I hate being cooped up in an office.''

Wade pulled the papers out of her hands and tossed everything into the big cardboard box that lay open under the stairs. "My priorities have changed, Clarissa. Why waste time on the past?''

She wanted to say something. Anything. She wanted to tell him that she had money enough to fulfill his dream, but that would be a lie. Belatedly she remembered the van. Why had she insisted on that van? If only she'd known about this!

Wade quickly heaved the rest of the boxes out of the way, lugged the give-away ones upstairs and helped her shift around some old leftover furniture so that they eventually created a kind of informal den. He said nothing while he did it, offered no words to explain, nothing that would help her understand or allow any commiseration.

"I think that should do it. It'll be all right for the kids, don't you think?" She looked to him for confirmation.

"It's fine. They can crash down here in comfort. These old cement basements never seem to get very warm, even on the hottest days.'' Wade glanced around once more. "Is there anything else that needs doing?''

"Not down here, no. I've got some painting in the girls' room that I'd like to get finished before they come back. And I want to clean the carpets, but I've got a whole week for that.'' She was babbling and she knew it, but Wade's face looked so odd. He seemed to be in another world.

"Oh." He stood at the bottom of the stairs, waiting for her to go first. By the time they were back in the kitchen the ominous rumble of thunderclouds could be heard rattling in the west. "We're going to get a storm."

"Good." Clarissa blew her bangs off her forehead as she poured them both a glass of iced tea. "It'll be that much nicer to work if it's cool." She pushed a glass across the table to him, then allowed herself to flop onto the closest chair, more tired than she was prepared to admit.

Wade sat across from her, fiddling with the moisture droplets on the outside of his glass as he stared at the ice cubes floating on the top.

Since she didn't know what to say, Clarissa remained silent, waiting for him to open up. The gap of quiet yawned between them, stretching her nerves taut. Something was wrong, she could feel it. Whenever he thought she wasn't looking, Wade stared at her as if she'd sprouted horns.

When she could stand it no longer, Clarissa cleared her throat, racking her brain for something to say. "Did you have anything—"

"Clarissa, would you mind if I left you alone for today? I need to do some thinking and it would help if I could get away from the phone for a while."

He didn't say "and you," but Clarissa was positive that's what he'd meant.

"Of course I don't mind! I suggested it, if you remember. Are you going to try golfing?" She flushed at her own obviousness. Why was it so important to know? Why was she still reminded of his uncle's insistence that Wade always ran away from his responsibilities?

"No, nothing like that. I just want to go somewhere quiet, get my brain straightened out. You have to admit that the past few months have been a little hectic." He smiled ruefully, as if to remind her of his words before they'd been married. "Unless you need me to help you with something around here? I could always go another time."

Clarissa heard the wistfulness in his voice and her heart melted. He just wanted a break, some time to himself. And why not? Hadn't he been working flat out since she'd met him? Wasn't this what love was all about—giving when the other person needed it?

She leaned across the table, her hand grasping his. "There's nothing that needs doing here," she told him sincerely, her eyes steady as they met his. "Go and relax. Take a break. You've earned it." She made herself summon a quirky little smile. "And to tell you the truth, it would be easier for me to get some work done if I didn't have to think about making you lunch and supper. Not that I'm trying to get rid of you, but..."

"Clarissa." His amused tone stopped her cold. "I get it. I'm in the way, and you wouldn't be averse to a little time spent on your own either. Nothing wrong with that."

It wasn't what she meant at all, but Clarissa let it go. Maybe believing that made it easier for him. So be it.

"No, nothing at all wrong with wanting some time

alone,'' she murmured, shutting down the pestering voice in her brain.

''Right.'' He swallowed his tea in one gulp, then pushed away from the table. ''I won't be late,'' he promised, bending over to brush his lips against hers. ''Or if I am, I'll call you. Okay?''

She nodded, afraid to ask what was really going through her mind. Why couldn't he talk to his wife? Why did he need to get away from her?

She watched as he picked up his sunglasses, the keys to his truck and then pulled out two cans of juice she'd put to cool in the fridge. ''Are you sure you don't want to take some brownies along?'' she offered, tongue in cheek.

Wade grinned, slicked a finger through the icing, licked it off with apparent delight, then slid the rest of the brownies into the trash. ''Thanks, anyway,'' he told her seriously. ''But I used all the antacids last night.'' He loped to the screen door and yanked it open. ''See you later, Clara.''

''Later,'' Clarissa repeated, wondering privately why it was that Wade always looked much happier to be leaving her than he did when coming home.

A few seconds later the rumble of his truck told her he was gone. She sighed and shoved to her feet, pushing a few straggling hairs back as a tiny breeze wafted in through the open window. Seconds later a light but steady rain began.

''Perfect painting weather,'' she told herself and leaned down to tug the cans out of the cupboard where she'd stored them. ''Now get to work.''

Chapter Eleven

The storm didn't hit Waseka directly. Most of the thunderclouds passed just to the south, bringing cooler air and life-giving moisture to the dry crops and wilting flowers. The lightning and thunder lit the sky from a distance, but Waseka sat calm and peaceful, as if in the eye of the storm.

Clarissa stood in front of the fan, letting it blow directly on her as she studied her work. The pink-tinged paint made a world of difference, giving the room a bright new look that was warm and inviting. She was considering curtains, bright candy-cane striped curtains she could make from that remnant of fabric she'd kept for so long, when the phone rang.

She hurried out in the hallway, wondering why painting one room was such an operation. "I'm out of shape," she told herself, with a dire look at her sweaty reflection. "Hello?"

"Is that Clarissa?"

"Yes, Mrs. Saltzburg, it's me. Is anything the matter?" Now she wished she'd let it ring.

"Yes, something is terribly the matter. My roof is leaking! Can you imagine? That storm rushed right by my place and took the shingles with it. I have buckets all over the place, and there's no end to it. Please have your husband come over immediately. I must have it fixed."

Ah, just desserts, decided Clarissa, stifling the tiny smile that rose to her lips. Then she gave herself a stiff lecture on loving those who needed it most.

"I am really sorry, Mrs. Saltzburg, but Wade isn't home. I don't expect him back until late tonight." She crossed her fingers for good measure, just in case. "Can you manage till tomorrow morning? Though I'm not sure he'll be able to do anything even then. I don't think they reroof when it's raining."

For the hundredth time Clarissa wished Wade had told her more about his business. How was she supposed to sound knowledgeable when she hadn't a clue about any of it?

"I don't see why he can't come over immediately. It's not as if he's doing anything special just because he's having coffee with that bunch of gossiping old men in the café. Saw him myself. If it were my day off, I wouldn't choose to spend it with those old fools."

Privately, Clarissa felt the same. She frowned. He'd wanted to get away to think, he'd said. Surely one couldn't do much deep thinking at the local watering hole.

"Well, either way, I'll let him know as soon as possible. Take care, Mrs. Saltzburg."

"Take care! Humph. As if I can with all these buckets lying helter-skelter. Beacock, this pail is full. Must I tell you—" The rest of the sentence was cut off with an abrupt click.

Clarissa whispered a prayer for the plight of poor Beacock as she replaced the phone. But her mind returned immediately to Wade. Some time with the boys, that's what he needed.

Her heart grew lighter as she reminded herself of the strawberries. They'd be all alone in the house tonight. Maybe she could...

Clarissa went back to the girls' bedroom and snapped the lids on the empty paint cans. It wouldn't be difficult to stitch up those drapes. Especially since she could set up her machine right here in this room. It wasn't a bad place to work at all, not with the breeze blowing lovely cool air in and the fan circulating air out the door.

She hurried down the stairs to get rid of the cans and wash out her supplies. She felt dizzy for a moment or two in the kitchen. It was because she'd bent down too quickly. Heat did that to you. Also hunger.

Her eyes widened as she noted that it was now after three. It didn't take a minute to help herself to a slice of ham and some of the potato salad she'd purchased that morning. She zapped the roll for a couple of seconds in her new microwave and licked her lips as the butter drizzled down into the soft fluffy flesh.

"Oh, this ham is excellent," she told Tabby, who strolled into the kitchen just long enough to sniff at her food. With a purr of disgust, the cat sauntered out of the room into the living room. Clarissa shrugged. "Be like that, then. I haven't had potato salad in ages."

Clarissa ate slowly, savoring each mouthful, her mind busy with the curtains. It felt good to relax for a while, to enjoy food she hadn't prepared or cleaned up after. She tried to remember when she'd eaten last, but couldn't.

"It's been too hot," she rationalized, remembering how weak she'd felt earlier. "Nobody can eat when it's hot."

Her stomach jerked and quivered in revulsion and Clarissa hurried to the bathroom. When she'd finally recovered, she returned to the table, pouring herself a glass of cool water that she sipped as she reached for the phone.

"Hello, Gerda? This is Clarissa Featherhawk. I bought some of that potato salad this morning, and I'm pretty sure it's off. I just ate some and I've been quite sick. I thought you might want to throw it out."

"I only made it this morning, Clarissa." Gerda's German accent grew stronger, her voice more indignant. "I haf served it to all my lunch customers vith no complaints. I don't sink dis is de problem, Clarissa."

"Oh. Well, the only other thing I had to eat was the ham and the bun and they both tasted fine." She'd been trying to warn her, but now Clarissa felt like an idiot for saying a word.

"Perhaps it is zee heat." Gerda's harsh tones softened. "Eet makes us all sick."

"Yes, that must be it. Sorry to have bothered

you." Clarissa hung up the phone, chiding herself for her impulsive act. Why had she disturbed that poor woman? Gerda was as careful of food poisoning as it was possible to be in a deli.

Once she'd finished her water, Clarissa felt better. It took only a few moments to set up the machine after she'd cut the material. Within two hours she had the curtains stitched and was just finishing hanging them when the phone rang again.

"Hello?"

"It's me." Wade sounded tired, dispirited. "I haven't gone anywhere yet. I'm waiting for someone. I'm not sure when I'll get home, Clarissa."

"Wade, it doesn't matter." She tried to be understanding, to cut him some slack, as Jared would say. "You don't have to check in with me. Just do whatever it is you need to do. I'm fine. In fact, I'm just hanging the drapes in the girls' room. Then I'm going to get the rug shampooer going."

"Don't wear yourself out. Maybe I should come home and give you a hand." He sounded depressed.

"It's your day off, Wade. Relax!"

She hung up the phone before he could argue.

After hanging the curtains and straightening the room, Clarissa took a coffee break.

She flopped into a kitchen chair and found herself drooping with fatigue. Eat something, her brain told her.

Clarissa moved to the fridge, her eyes moving from the cold cuts to the salad, to the strawberries. Ah, that was just the thing. With a little ice cream.

She leaned against the counter as she rinsed off

several of the plump ripe berries and dished up a tiny scoop of lemon sherbet.

The berries were tangy, their flavor making her tongue come alive. She'd eaten three, and one spoonful of sherbet, before her queasy stomach rebelled.

"What a terrible time to get the flu," she muttered, emerging from the bathroom, clutching a cold wet washcloth to her forehead.

She sank back into her chair, shoving the food away as the phone rang for the third time. "Yes?" she asked with a sigh.

"Ya, Gerda here. Das ist Clarissa?"

"Yes. Hello, Gerda." Clarissa forced her head to stay up when all she wanted to do was lay it on her arms and go to sleep.

"You are okay? No more sick?"

Clarissa wished a thousand times over that she'd never made that phone call. How embarrassing! Now the whole town would know she'd maligned the kindhearted woman.

"I'm fine, Gerda. Thanks for asking."

"Ach, you do not sound fine." Gerda's snort of disapproval carried clearly across the line. "I think you haf been sick again, yes?"

"Yes," Clarissa admitted. "It must be some kind of flu. I only had a few bites of strawberries, but that was all it took."

"*Nein, das* is *nicht* flu." Gerda's harsh voice softened. "*Das ist eine* baby."

"I'm sorry, I didn't quite catch that." Clarissa shook her head, trying to stay awake. "What did you say?"

"A baby, Clarissa. You are waiting for a baby?"

Clarissa gulped, her eyes widening until she could see nothing but stars. She blinked once, then answered the urgent summons from the receiver in her hand.

"Yes, I'm here. But I think I have to go now, Gerda. I'm sure you're wrong, though." She almost replaced the receiver, then thought of something. "Have you seen Wade, Gerda?"

"Yah. He vas here mit zee pastor. Talking, talking." She called something out to someone else, then returned to the conversation. "He's gone. You rest, Clarissa. And get better. When babies come, you must be healthy."

"Yes, of course. Thank you. Goodbye." She hung up the phone, then went to stand at the screen so the evening air could cool her heated face.

It couldn't be? Could it? Clarissa tried to remember, tried to figure dates and such, but nothing would stay in her head. The plain truth was, she didn't know. It *could* happen.

Oh, but wouldn't it be wonderful if she was. A baby! A precious tiny baby she could hold in her arms, share with the children. A tiny prayer answered.

She touched her stomach with wonder. Could it be?

Of all the prayers she'd prayed, this was the one she'd been remiss in repeating. There hadn't been time to think about babies lately. She'd been too busy with the children, the library, learning to love Wade.

Wade!

The joy drained away just as the rain followed a little rivulet on its way to the gutter at the end of her walk. How terrible for Wade! He didn't want more responsibility, didn't want another person dependent on him, holding him back from the dreams that were far bigger than anything Clarissa had suspected.

Wade, who needed freedom, time to think, a place to be alone, how could she expect him to be excited about this? It would only be another burden, a burden she'd put on him. He'd feel trapped by their marriage, trapped by her. She and the baby could become another chore, another "to-do" on his list of "have-tos."

The whole, unbearable weight of it dragged her shoulders down, pressed against her forehead until it ached. Why hadn't she thought ahead, considered this? Done something to prevent it?

A little coo of sheer bliss echoed through her mind, the picture of tiny fat fingers reaching out flashed before her eyes. Such a precious thing, a baby. Such a joy to behold as it grew to know and understand its world.

She thrust it away, all of it, as Wade's dark brooding eyes swam into their place. The shuttered look he hid behind this afternoon when he'd glanced at the acceptance form from the admissions board. That desperate shove that sent an old and tattered blue bankbook with a zero balance into the trash box when he thought she wasn't looking. The hasty burial of drafting pencils and T squares under children's clothes.

That picture was replaced by one of herself, huge and ungainly as she tried to maneuver around the kitchen to get dinner on as Wade waited tiredly amid a mess that she couldn't get cleaned up. She saw him dragging in, day after day, handing over his paycheck before he went to wash up, jeans tattered and torn, filthy with plaster dust.

And his hair, his beautiful jet-wing hair, no longer glossy, but lackluster and thinning, more silver than black as it lay cropped and shingled against his head.

"Oh, Lord, help me." She let the tears fall then, hot bitter tears for a future that could never be. "Please don't let me be pregnant," she whispered, the agony of uttering those words tearing at her heart until her entire body mourned. "He doesn't want more responsibilities, more burdens to shoulder. He's such a good man and all he wants is to fulfill his dream. Is that so wrong?"

She stepped outside, onto the back step and let the little spits of rain dash against her hot cheeks.

"He's a good man, a wonderful husband and father. But he's nervous about responsibility. And no wonder. He had to take it on so young." She thought about the dream that had been stashed away under the stairwell. "I'd give almost anything for him to go back to school."

God is in control.

She looked up at the darkening sky, almost certain she'd heard a voice. "I know. And You always make the right decisions."

Trust in the Lord.

"I do, God. I trust You so much." She gulped down the huge lump in the middle of her throat and gave up what she'd always longed for. "But God, if You need me to, I can give up my dream for Wade's. It was a silly, fairy-tale dream anyway." She choked down the sob, but continued. "I've already got four wonderful kids to look after, to cherish, to raise for You.'' She squeezed her hands together, knowing what she had to do.

''I don't need a baby, Lord. What Wade needs is far more important than me and I don't ever want to make him feel I'm draining him.''

Clarissa waited for an answer, a sign that would tell her what to do next. As she did, a scene from the past paraded through her mind. She was ten and looking forward to two weeks of camp. She loved camp and this year it would be doubly exciting because Gran was going to Scotland while she was gone. A sister still lived there, they'd corresponded for months.

Clarissa remembered the excitement she'd found gazing at travel brochures and watching her grandmother's eyes light up as she came upon a favorite place she remembered from her childhood. They'd spent hours pouring over maps, guidebooks, the letters, making sure each detail was carefully organized. It was the trip of a lifetime.

Then, the morning before Clarissa was to leave, the trip was off. Gran simply said her sister needed more time to prepare, but Clarissa knew it was more than that. She'd puzzled over it for hours, sitting there on the veranda as the rain spattered the garden. And then she'd heard the telephone conversation that had changed her life. Gran was explaining why she wouldn't be coming to Celia, her sister.

''I'm sorry, dear, but I just can't manage it this year. Clarissa has to have braces and there's only my savings to pay for them. No, don't cry, Celia. I will get there, I promise. Just not this summer. Clarissa's needs come first. The dentist says the bite must be corrected as soon as possible or she'll have lifelong problems.'' Her Gran's voice stopped, waited a moment, then continued.

''No, she doesn't know. And I won't tell her why. It's not her fault.''

Clarissa remembered the choking sob, then the softly spoken words. ''But, oh Celia, I wanted so badly to see you again. Just for a while.''

That's when the truth had dawned. She, Clarissa, was a burden. She was stopping Gran from doing things, from seeing the one person left from her family. How many times had it happened since she'd come here? How many other times had Gran done without, given up some dream she held so precious, just because Clarissa had come along?

As a child, Clarissa prayed and prayed for an answer, but none came. She'd gone off to camp with a sore spot on her soul. She'd stayed only one week that year. One miserable, lonely week while she made up her mind never to be a burden again.

Clarissa winced back to the present. ''What am I going to do, Lord?'' she whispered, pushing away her yearning for a baby.

The answer rumbled through her mind, a verse learned at camp.

Be still and know that I am God.

She knew that. She was confident that God could do anything. But how could He possibly straighten out this mess? Either way, she or Wade would lose the one thing they really wanted, wouldn't they?

Chapter Twelve

"I'm sorry to bother you." Wade tugged off his cap and shoved it into the back pocket of his jeans. "I know you're busy with important things and I'm probably wasting your time, but..."

"But you needed to talk to someone." The pastor grinned and motioned toward a kitchen chair. "I'm just glad I got home before you left. Want some coffee?"

"Sure." Wade slumped into the chair at the same time as he ordered his weary body to get out of there. When had he ever spilled his guts to anyone? He sure didn't need to start now, at the ripe old age of thirty. And yet he did.

"Actually, I'm starving. Mind if I scramble some eggs? I can do some for you, too, if you're hungry." The pastor waited for Wade's nod, then pulled out a frypan and began cracking eggs. "So what's up in your busy family?"

"The kids are off at camp. Clarissa took a week

off so she could get some housecleaning done. Everything's fine.'' Wade shuffled his feet nervously. "Look, Pastor—"

"It's Michael, or Mike to my friends. Which I hope you intend to be.'' He grinned in exactly the same way Pierce did when he was trying to con you into something.

"Okay, Mike." Wade squeezed his eyes shut, took a deep breath and blew it out on a sigh. "I don't know how to say this. No matter which way I phrase it, it's going to come out wrong."

"Why don't you just tell me what's eating at you and stop waiting for someone to judge?" Mike stirred his eggs with one hand while the other popped bread into the toaster. "I'm listening."

"It's Clarissa. No, it's me. Actually it's both of us." Wade shook his head, frustration welling up inside. "I didn't marry her because I loved her," he blurted out in a rush of air and then proceeded to tell the pastor the reason why they'd married.

Mike handed him the butter and the toast. "Here, you can do this." He turned back to the eggs. "So?"

"Well, the thing is, I think I committed a sin by doing that. A mighty big one." Wade knew his face was beet-red so he kept his head down, his eyes on his task.

"A sin?" Mike let out a belly laugh. "Well, brother, if you think making a home for four needy kids with a woman as loving as Clarissa is a sin, you've got a strange idea of God."

"I do?" Wade thought about that. "Yeah, probably I do. I never had much of a father figure in my dad, you know. I always kinda pictured God as this judge sort of fellow, who laid out a bunch of laws and waited to see who would keep them. I don't think even your kind of benevolent God would approve of my selfishness when it comes to Clarissa. No one would.''

"What is this 'my God, your God' garbage?'' Mike leaned backward, grabbed the coffeepot and filled two cups. "There is only one God, buddy. And He's the God of love.''

"Love!'' Wade flung down his fork. "That's what started this whole mixed-up mess,'' he sputtered. "I can't love anyone.''

"Oh?'' Mike quirked one eyebrow, his jaws crunching the toast. "Why's that?''

Wade felt a rush of anger like he'd never experienced before. Why was he here anyway? What good would it do to maul it all over with someone who so patently didn't understand?

"If you don't let it out, I can't help.'' The chiding voice got to him.

"Fine.'' Flinging down his napkin, Wade jumped to his feet, paced out the black-and-white kitchen tiles, then paced back again. He stopped right beside Mike's chair. "Anybody I love gets hurt. Doesn't matter that I don't want that, that I try to do the best. It always goes wrong.''

"Mm-hm.'' Mike took a slug of coffee, helped himself to another lump of egg, then cocked his head to one side. "Why is that?''

"Because they always want something from me and I have nothing to give,'' he snapped out, angered by the other man's cavalier approach. "I get scared by all those demands and then I do something stupid or take off. I just can't handle other people's expectations.''

"Running away?" Mike nodded. "I know about that.''

Wade snickered. "Yeah, I'm sure, Pastor.''

"Think not?" Mike was calm, his eyes steady. "Think about this. Ten years ago I was fourteen. I hot-wired a car and took it for a joyride. Crashed.''

Wade flopped back down into his chair, his attention caught by the calm recital. "You?''

Mike nodded. "Me," he confirmed. "My parents had a cabin at the lake, and I hid out there as long as I could, knowing what the right thing to do was, but scared spitless to own up to my mistakes.''

Wade wasn't exactly sure what protocol in this situation was. Should he ask Mike to continue, even though it was no doubt very painful?

"You don't have to look at me like that. I can talk about it now. It helps to know that at least I learned something from the incident." He grinned, his quirky mouth offering a wry smile.

"Okay, I'll bite. What did you learn?" Wade picked at his egg, but his interest wasn't in food. He reached for his cup, but his hand stopped midway at the response.

"I learned about grace.''

He gulped. Now for the sermon, he thought to himself. "That was her name?''

Mike shook his head. "Uh-uh. That was the lesson. Her name was Margaret. Margaret Milton. She was seventy-one and about as big as a wasp. But could she sting!" He chuckled in remembrance. "The accident meant she had to take a cab to do meals-on-wheels. But that didn't slow her down one whit. She made her presence felt by contacting the police and the judge. She refused to press charges, said she'd drum up a real ruckus unless she could have some say in what my punishment would be.

"I was sure she was up to something, but she was so friendly, I hung around. Margaret insisted I'd been given an opportunity. She said she loved God, that He controlled her life and everything to do with it. She insisted that it had to be His will that I stole her car so something good could come of it." Mike grinned. "I figured she was off her rocker, but if it would keep me out of jail, I was all for it. I shut up and listened."

"She does sound a little loony," Wade agreed.

"But that's just it, she wasn't. She totally believed that God was in control and she did the best she could with what He gave her. She said she'd learned love that way and that evidently I was to be her next project. I laughed my head off, but I couldn't avoid hearing more of her theories. I had to keep going back there or wait in jail. I chose Margaret."

"I suppose she forced you to do a lot of stuff around her house or something, to pay off the debt?" Wade had met those kind of do-gooders before, those upright souls who were bent on exacting revenge.

"Nope, all she did was insist that I do a Bible study with her. I'd been to church, I figured I knew what most of it meant, so I agreed. We met three times a week, to talk over what we'd studied. But she wouldn't get off I Corinthians 13."

"The 'Love' chapter." Wade sighed, closing his

eyes for just a moment as he remembered the night Clarissa had read those words to him.

"You got it. Love, love, love. That's all I heard for three long months. Every Monday, Wednesday and Friday evening I'd go over, and we'd talk about it. The more we talked, the more I realized that love isn't an action, it's a process. It's not something you do like speaking wisdom, or moving mountains. You see, you can do all those things without love."

"I get it. Like where it says giving to the poor, or having your body burned." Wade nodded.

"Yes. You can do all that, but if you don't love, it doesn't matter a whit." Mike leaned forward, his hand reaching across the table for his big black Bible. He flipped through it quickly, finding the passage he sought. "After he says that, Paul goes on to tell us what love looks like. It's long-suffering, kind, doesn't envy, isn't boastful or proud, doesn't behave poorly, can't be easily provoked. See here." He slid his finger along the passage.

"Thinks no evil, rejoices in the truth, bears all things, believes all things, hopes all things, endures all things." To Wade it sounded exactly like Clarissa. She lived what these verses talked about.

Mike pulled the Bible back in front of him. "But it goes on. It tells us that the only thing that will last is love. Everything else, even the good things, will pass away."

"I know all that. You spoke on it a couple of weeks ago." Wade wondered for the tenth time why he'd come here. It was an interesting story, but he was looking for help, not stories. "The thing is, I'm no good at love. I'm not dependable. In fact, I'm not any of those things you just listed.'' He made a face.

''I get to feeling like I'm boxed in and I can only think of being free. What good would it do Clarissa if I loved her, Mike? She doesn't need me putting more demands on her. She's already working herself to a shadow trying to prove that running a home, keeping four kids on the ball and working aren't too much for her.''

Mike opened his mouth, but shut it abruptly when Wade spoke again.

''I keep hoping we'll get a moment together, some time and space to work things out, to talk about what we want the future to bring, what she wants from me, what she expects me to do. But she's always got another job, another load of laundry, another little talk to have with the kids.'' He laughed bitterly. ''Ironic, isn't it? That's exactly why I married her. Fool that I am, I thought that would be enough, for her and for me.''

''And it's not?'' Mike carried the dishes to the sink and ran hot water over them.

Wade was grateful for the break, it gave him time to organize what he was trying to explain.

''No!'' he blurted out at last. ''She says she loves me, and I believe her. But at the same time, I don't want her to.''

''Why?''

''Because it makes me indebted to her. I only ever hurt the people I care most about. And I don't ever want to hurt Clarissa. She doesn't deserve that. No one does.''

Mike flopped into the chair and hooted with laughter. "That's a crock, Wade, and you know it."

Wade flushed, stung by the reproof in those tones. "I don't know what you mean."

"Sure you do." He waited a moment, then sighed. "Okay, I'll lay it out for you, buddy. You're a fraidy cat." Mike fixed his gaze on him and dared him to look away. "You want Clarissa to love you, you bask in all the attention she pays you. You like hearing the folks say what a wonderful couple you make, how the kids look so cared for and her house seems to hum. You love it when she tells people how careful you are at your job."

"I didn't know she did that," he mumbled, his cheeks burning, but then Wade recalled a certain telephone call and knew he lied.

"Oh, you know, buddy. You just won't admit it to yourself. Because then you'd have to respond and you're too wrapped up in yourself to reach out. At least, that's what you're telling yourself."

"You make me sound like a first-class creep," Wade muttered, grinding his back teeth together when what he really wanted was to hit something.

"Isn't that what you just told me you are?" Mike put a hand on his arm. "Listen to me, Wade. Love isn't about doing things. I know you've done a thousand things to repay her for taking you and the kids on. That's not the issue."

"It's exactly the issue!" Wade exploded. "Don't you see that it doesn't matter what I do! How am I supposed to repay her for the eyestrain she gets when she spends hours sewing sequins on a costume for school? How can I possibly do anything that will compensate her for the days she's spent building up Pierce's self-esteem or teaching Tildy to stop burning everything she touches? How—''

''You can't,'' Mike interrupted, calmly sipping his coffee.

Wade stared. It wasn't the answer he wanted. ''I don't...''

''It doesn't matter how long it takes you or how hard you try, Clarissa will never get back those hours she's spent, or the words she's shared. You can't repay her, Wade. And if I know Clarissa, she wouldn't want you to try.''

''Yes, but it's not fair.''

''Love isn't fair. It goes above and beyond the call of duty. It does things just because. It's a heart condition, Wade. Not an outward show, just a steady glowing thing inside the heart that makes you take the second step, push a little harder, work a little longer.''

''I can't accept that,'' Wade told him. ''There has to be something I can do to repay her.''

''You can do something.''

''What?'' At last they were getting somewhere. Wade moved to the edge of his chair and waited expectantly. ''What can I do?''

''Accept it.'' Mike smiled. ''It's called grace, Wade. And it works the same way as God does with us. Do you think it benefits Him to have human beings who keep running to Him for every little pimple? No. It's just more work. But He loves it when we keep coming to Him.'' He grinned.

''Do you think it benefits you to slave away like a fool so you can earn enough money for Pierce to be on the baseball team or Lacey to buy a new dress for the prom? Wouldn't you be far better off to keep your money and take yourself on a nice little holiday?''

Wade frowned. ''But I want to do those things. I love doing things for them. They're my kids.''

''I know. And that's exactly how God is with us. We bawl all over His shoulder, we nag Him for things that we shouldn't have, things that will make us sick or cause us problems, and He answers our prayers because He loves us. It causes Him more work to help us pick up the pieces after, but He stays right there.''

''And you're saying that's how it is with Clarissa? That she only does what she does because she loves us.'' Wade thought about that for a moment.

''Well, maybe not everything. Some things just have to get done and you close your eyes, bite your lip and do them.'' Mike smirked as he jerked a thumb toward the sink. ''That's how I feel about dishes. But I like to eat off clean plates so I wash them. Or cadge my friends to do 'em.'' His meaning was unmistakable.

Wade got up, ran some water and squirted in a blob of detergent. ''So, how does this have anything to do with me loving Clarissa?'' he asked finally, his brain whirling in confusion at these new concepts.

''It has everything to do with it. God sent you here, Wade. He sent you Clarissa, too. I'm convinced of that. He blessed you with a wife and a family that any man in this town would be proud to call his own.''

''I know how great she is. And I'm grateful.''

Wade rinsed the plates and laid them on the tea towel. "But..."

"But you want to whine and complain because God went and put some love in her heart for you that you might have to accept. You want to dwell in the past, linger over your past failures, savor the hurt and the pain a little longer?" Mike stayed where he was, watching Wade as he began drying the few utensils they'd used. "You'd rather think about the past than face up to what the future could hold. Isn't that what's at the bottom of this?"

It wasn't a pretty picture, and Wade didn't dwell on it.

"What if something bad comes up?" he challenged. "What if I do or say something, hurt her somehow? What am I supposed to do then?" Wade couldn't tolerate the thought of Clarissa being hurt by his stupidity. "Isn't it just better to avoid it?"

"Avoid what? Life? Love?" Mike shook his head. "You can't do it, man. And if you try, you'd be telling the world a lie. Isn't your God big enough to handle whatever comes up in your lives? Can't He forgive you for past sins and teach you new things? Isn't it possible that God has a perfect plan laid out just for you, a blueprint of how your life should be from here on in?"

"I never thought of that." Wade tossed the towel onto the counter. He could imagine the analogy very well, he just didn't know how to find that blueprint.

"Read your Bible. Love is a state of the heart, Wade. But when love is there, actions follow. The things Clarissa has done have shown the love inside her. You can't see it, but you know it's there because of the way she acts. How about you? Have you shown her any love?''

Wade felt his face burn again, but he made himself say the words. ''I can't seem to tell her what I'm feeling,'' he mumbled.

''She doesn't need the words as much as she needs to see what's in your heart. Look at this, Wade. Maybe it will help. Paul wrote it after the love passage. 'When I was a child I spoke and thought and reasoned as a child does. But when I became a man, my thoughts grew far beyond those of my childhood, and now I have put away childish things.' You see?''

Wade grimaced, but his heart felt twenty times lighter. ''What you're telling me is that I need to grow up. Right?''

''Mm, basically, yes.'' Mike grinned. ''Growing up means you give up some silly childish fantasies of what life should be like, give up the idea of getting even for past slights, and start making your life match God's blueprint. You build it into what He wants it to be.''

''If I just knew what that was.'' Wade snagged his jacket and pulled it on slowly. ''I thought I knew what I wanted, but now things look different to me. As if I can't quite see the whole picture. If only I could get my mind cleared and in tune with His.''

''It just so happens, I have the perfect way for you to start doing that.'' Mike pulled a key ring out of his pocket and tossed it across. ''Take this. I've got a little shack, a rough cabin, that's back in the woods a ways. Why don't you go out there for a day or two and sort things out with God?''

''Sort things out? You mean like fall on my face,

or something?'' Wade didn't think he wanted more emotionalism. He wanted good, rational reasoning, a way to handle his problems that didn't mean welching on his commitments.

Mike raised his eyebrows. "Well, buddy, if that's the way you think best, go for it. You just have to ask, and He will make the path perfectly clear." He smirked slyly. "Personally, I always think He speaks more clearly when I'm sitting on the end of the dock, dangling a line in the water."

Wade wanted to go so badly, he could almost taste it. To be able to think things through, to consider what marriage to Clarissa really involved, to ponder the future—one without the architectural degree he'd craved so long. Some time alone to relax and listen for a heavenly answer to his earthly fears.

Then he thought of Clarissa home alone, waiting for him. She was sitting at home right now, carrying the load that was rightfully his. "I'd really like to go, Mike, but I'll need to check with Clarissa first."

"Of course. Here's a map. I drew it for a buddy of mine who never showed. Take as long as you need, Wade. I'll be praying for you."

Wade nodded, thanked him and hurried out the door. The rain was pouring down in sheets now, but he barely noticed as he headed for home.

Funny to think of that old monstrosity as home, to feel a little flutter of warmth amid the icy coldness that clamped his insides. But he did. He, who'd sworn never to settle down, couldn't remember when he'd last thought of a place as home. Was that because Clarissa was there, waiting?

"I don't know what You have in store for me,"

he murmured, as he pulled into the driveway and noted the light Clarissa had left burning for him. "But I'd like to. Please show me how to go about this. And remember I'm as dumb as a stump when it comes to women."

The house was dark, save for the stove light that cast glimmering shadows in the kitchen. Wade locked up, then climbed the stairs, marveling at the sense of rightness that settled on him with each upward step. He'd wanted to design homes with just this ambience, places where people could be exactly who they wanted. Places where people were loved, cared for, unafraid to say what they wanted, needed from someone else.

Was that dream totally dead? It was just another question that he needed an answer to.

In the bedroom, Clarissa lay curled up on her side of the bed, fast asleep. He showered, then climbed in beside her, his arms wrapping around her slim body, snuggling her against him. Clarissa shifted but didn't waken. Wade kissed her cheek, noting the shadows under her eyes and the lines of tiredness around her mouth. He wished he'd spent the day with her.

"We'll have other days," he promised softly. "I've just got to get a few things ironed out with God and then you and I are going to have a heart-to-heart—with no children to interrupt."

He didn't know exactly what he'd say, how he'd explain the roiling misgivings that churned inside his brain. But he'd pray about it. With his chin on her hair, Wade lay in the darkness and thought about his wife. He remembered how she'd cut his hair last week, her fingers light, tender as she'd snipped and cut, her bottom lip caught between her teeth as she concentrated.

The days he'd come home with his hands aching from tearing up a floor that should never have been laid, she'd insisted on setting aside supper preparations to bathe and bandage his bruised and battered knuckles, carefully removing the splinters and slivers as tears rolled down her cheeks. He could almost hear her soft eyes and sympathetic voice as she'd talked with Pierce and Lacey last night, answering their tearful questions about heaven and whether their parents were able to see them.

I want to be a part of that. I want to be there, to support her, to help her deal with them. They're my family. Clarissa is my wife. I don't know why, but she loves me. I can't let that go. Maybe I should, but I can't. It's too precious, too priceless.

He was going to fight off this restlessness, Wade realized as the raindrops spattered against the window. He was going to ask God some hard questions and he intended to listen until he got some answers.

Clarissa and her love are a once-in-a-lifetime gift that everyone doesn't get. And You gave them to me. It's time I realized what that gift entails and did something about returning it, or get out of her way. Clarissa isn't like anyone else. I can trust her, talk to her about my fears. She'll understand.

Clarissa's hand slid up his chest and cupped his cheek. "Wade?" she murmured, still mostly asleep.

"It's me, honey. Go back to sleep."

She smiled that angelic look that caught at his heart and made his breath catch. Her fingers brushed across his lips in a featherlight touch of assurance as she snuggled a little closer. "I love you, Wade," she murmured, her whispery soft voice trailing away into dreamland with the last syllable.

"I know," he told her quietly. "Thank you."

"Welcome." Her breathing returned to its regular pattern.

But Wade lay awake, cherishing this precious gift he'd been given even as he asked the Father how he could ever accept it.

He wasn't the kind of man someone like Clarissa needed. He was all wrong for her. And if he had any brains, he'd get out before he spoiled all their lives.

Before he ruined whatever bit of feeling she would have left if she knew how badly he wanted to run and keep on running.

Chapter Thirteen

Clarissa woke up the next morning when a sunbeam twinkled across her face. Bemused, she reached out a hand, but Wade's side of the bed was empty. As usual. Instead, her fingers crunched against a bit of paper he'd torn from the pad on the night table and left on his pillow.

She sat up, frowned, then unfolded the note.

Clarissa. I need to get away, just for a bit to think things through. I'm fine, I just have some important decisions to make. If you need me, contact the pastor. He'll know where I am. Wade.

Her stomach squeezed itself into a knot. He had to get away? From her? From responsibility? Which one? And why now? Why, when they could have spent some time together, had he taken off to a place he didn't even want to talk about?

"Lord, I don't want to complain, but this really isn't the kind of marriage I had in mind."

She swung her legs out of bed and then reeled as

her stomach issued an urgent summons. Suddenly yesterday's events came rushing back as she raced for the bathroom.

Half an hour later she was cleaned up and in the van, heading for the supermarket out on highway 97, where no one knew her personally. She purchased the pregnancy kit, two oranges and a quart of milk, then hurried home. Less than fifteen minutes after flying up the stairs she flopped against the bathroom vanity, the blood draining from her legs. She had her answer.

Pregnant! Oh, why hadn't Wade waited? Why hadn't he stuck around so she could talk this over with him?

The phone rang and she grabbed it, praying it was him.

"Hi, Clarissa. It's Candy at Dr. Baker's office. You asked me to let you know if we had a cancellation and we do. I know your appointment is for next week, but if you want to come in right away, we can get that physical over with today."

She'd completely forgotten the library board's insistence on her having a yearly physical to qualify for their medical coverage.

"Thank you, Lord," she whispered.

Perhaps she was wrong. Perhaps she'd done the test wrong. Surely the doctor would find something noticeable if she was pregnant.

"Yes, I'll come right over. The kids are at camp and Wade's away, so it happens that I'm free."

She decided on the drive over that she wouldn't say anything. If Dr. Baker noticed some changes in her body, surely he'd tell her. It would be a confirmation, and she wouldn't look a fool if she asked to have a test done. Especially if it came back negative. Her lips pursed. If she wasn't pregnant, she was going to ask the good doctor about preventing that in the future, in spite of her own almost desperate craving for a baby. Wade's needs came before hers.

Dr. Baker had been practicing for years. He took his time with each patient and she was no different. When Clarissa had been fully examined, he told her to dress and then come into his office.

"Clarissa, your body has undergone some changes. I have a hunch you know what I'm going to say. I think you're pregnant, but I'd like to do a test."

"I suspected as much." She kept her eyes trained on his face. She'd known this man for years and something was bothering him.

Dr. Baker scratched his forehead. "There's something odd that's twigging at me, sort of trying to get my attention. I can't put my finger on it just yet, but I'd like to take all the precautions I can."

"Of course." She waited while they drew blood, then sat in the office chair while his lab nurse did her work. By the time she was called back into his office, Clarissa was a bundle of nerves.

"Definitely pregnant," he told her with a grin, his weathered face wreathed in a grin of happiness as he pumped her arm up and down in a hearty handshake. "Congratulations. I've made an appointment for you to have an ultrasound. Will around two be okay?"

She nodded, thanked him for his good wishes and went back home, her mind twisting and turning over the information. It should have been the happiest day of her life and yet on the inside she wept for the loss of Wade's dream.

"It's not that I don't want the baby," she told the Lord. "I can hardly wait. But, oh, God, how can I tell him? How can I burden him even more, when he's obviously already in a lot of turmoil?"

She thought of going to see her pastor, but in the end she decided not to. She would wait on God. He would see her through.

"Would you excuse me just a moment?" The technician at the hospital flicked a switch that turned the screen off and put the paddle back on the table. "I just need to speak to someone."

"Is anything wrong?" Clarissa asked, but the woman merely smiled and hurried out the door, her manner distracted.

"Oh, Lord, please help me. I'm so scared." Clarissa scrunched her eyes closed and prayed as hard as she ever had. "I know it's not the best timing, and I know Wade isn't going to like it, but God, I really want this baby. Please, please, let everything be all right." She hardly dared ask, "Can't I have both Wade and the baby?"

She felt as if she'd lain there for hours before the door burst open. A tall thin man with thick bleary glasses and an impatient step followed the technician into the room. Behind them came Dr. Baker.

"Please tell me what's wrong," Clarissa begged. "Please."

"Now, now." Doctor Baker patted her hand. "There's nothing wrong. Our Penny only wanted to check something out with her boss. Since I was here anyhow, I thought I'd tag along. Just relax, Clarissa. Close your eyes if you want to.''

But Clarissa kept them wide-open and focused on the screen, straining to see what it was that had the tall thin man studying it so intently. She knew Dr. Baker should be in his office right now. He had appointments. Penny had no doubt summoned him over, which meant that something was terribly wrong. Didn't it?

Finally, the ultrasound was done and Dr. Baker asked Penny to bring Clarissa to his office.

Clarissa sat in the office, impatiently fidgeting as she waited. Eventually the radiologist and Dr. Baker came in, heads together as they muttered indistinguishable medical words. Dr. Baker shoved the door closed, then sat down beside her and took her hands in his.

"Clarissa my dear, Dr. Grant and I are in agreement over your diagnosis."

"I thought I was pregnant," Clarissa mumbled, not understanding the knowing look that passed between the two men. "Is something else wrong?"

"No, no. It's not that. Is Wade here with you?"

"No, Dr. Baker. He's out of town for a while. Why? Please, will you just tell me what's wrong?" She was getting tired of this runaround.

"Nothing's wrong." Clearly Dr. Grant didn't hold with prolonging the suspense. "You're carrying twins. At least I'm ninety-nine percent certain it's twins."

"T-twins?" Clarissa sputtered, feeling her heart begin to race as the blood rushed out of her head. "Did you say twins? As in two babies?"

"We're fairly certain." Dr. Grant nodded at Dr. Baker.

"Oh, my! Oh, my goodness me." Clarissa let her mind drift for a minute, seeing two little cherubs flutter across the ceiling, the fat little hands entwined, their rosebud mouths grinning at her. "Oh, dear." She remembered Wade. "Ohh!"

"It is a bit of a shock, isn't it? I haven't delivered a set of twins in years. I'm rather looking forward to this. Will Wade be surprised, do you think?" Dr. Baker grinned like a cat who'd just spied some thick cream.

"Will he ever!" Clarissa's knees wobbled at the very thought. She glanced from one man to the other. "Do you think you can keep this quiet until I have a chance to tell him? I know what a hotbed of gossip this place is and I'd like to be the one he hears it from first."

"Everything that happens in this hospital is confidential," the radiologist told her, obviously upset by her accusatory words. "We do not gossip about our patients."

"Yeah, right." Clarissa gathered up her purse, her eyes on Dr. Baker. "Please? Will you keep it quiet? I'm not sure just when he'll be back."

"I'll speak to Penny immediately. We'll do the best we can, Clarissa, but I know I speak for the entire town when I tell you that it couldn't have happened to a nicer woman. You'll be just as wonderful with these babies as you are with Wade's kids. Your family will be the envy of everyone."

"Will it?" Clarissa thanked them and left the office, the hospital, with the words ringing around in her brain.

Her family. *Her* family. It was, wasn't it?

Twins? Twins! She wanted to jump for joy and praise God for answering her prayer. But at the same time she was so afraid of telling Wade, of seeing that dull, tired look wash into his eyes when he realized what she'd caused him to lose, what she was forcing him to accept. Wade wasn't a family man. Hadn't he told her that over and over?

"I will not doubt Your will," she whispered at last, leaning back in the recliner at home with a glass of iced tea nearby. "You have everything under control. You and You alone know how we'll manage, but I'll trust."

Wade had been gone almost two full days, and Clarissa was worried. She'd lain awake last night, her body craving sleep while her mind relived all the things she knew about Wade.

And one fact kept surfacing. Wade had left his mother and his sister, ran away when they needed him. He'd left again at seventeen.

Was he going to come back this time?

She spent her daylight hours accomplishing the items on her list, checking them off with no sense of satisfaction as one after the other was completed. The house gleamed from its polishing, the floors were spotless, the furniture without a speck of dust. The garden was weed-free, and the freezer held a host of ready-to-cook dinners and baking enough to last at least a week, even with four hungry children around.

Several ladies from the church brought over the

baking and Clarissa accepted it gratefully, wrapping
and freezing every bit. Evidently Dr. Baker's promise couldn't hold back the good souls of Waseka. It
seemed that everyone knew of her condition and
wanted to help. Wade would hate it, call it charity,
but she accepted each and every offer that was made.

Right now there was a crew of four workers outside painting the fence, and two more downstairs
checking out the furnace and water heater. A young
girl who'd sometimes helped her at the library offered to pick the peas while her boyfriend trimmed
the hedge and mowed the lawn. For Clarissa there
was nothing to do but sit and watch the hustle of
activity around her home and wonder where Wade
was, and what he was doing.

Chapter Fourteen

Half an hour later, Clarissa could have burst into song when her substitute at the library phoned to say she was having difficulty with the computer system. A little mental labor was just what she needed to get her mind off her problems.

Edna Morton had been the librarian before Clarissa and she didn't believe in computers. After all, she'd managed the library for years without it, why change?

"Just look at this pile of books I have to check out!" she shrieked when Clarissa finally walked through the big oak front door.

Thirty-five heads turned to stare at Clarissa. Thirty-five sets of impatient eyes watched as she stored her purse under the counter, then she picked up the stamp and waited for Bertha MacDonald to present her card.

"Back at work already, Clarissa? I thought you were on holidays or something?" Bertha shook her head, her double chins wagging her disgust. "I don't understand this new idea of taking separate holidays—Wade off at some cabin and you here, slaving over that house. Doesn't seem hardly fair. Especially not with you expecting and all."

Clarissa mentally groaned but forced a bright smile to her lips as a library full of interested parties widened their eyes and digested this newest bit of information.

"Oh, it's not really a holiday. And I'm not slaving over anything! Besides, we each have our jobs to do. We're married, but we're not siamese twins!" She giggled as if she had no more interest in being with Wade right now than fly to the moon.

"I guess." Bertha looked as if she didn't quite understand that reasoning, but thankfully she said nothing more. She stuffed her books into her bag and waddled out of the library.

And so it went, on and on, each one with a question, a hint, a suggestion on life after the honeymoon. By the time the last customer had left, Clarissa was hot and sticky and desperately tired. But the computer still sat, blank and useless. She had to get it running right away, or there would be a huge backlog of work when she came back. As tired as she felt now, it would only get worse.

With a sigh, Clarissa pulled out her book of emergency phone numbers and dialed. "Hello, Kyle. It's Clarissa Cart—I mean, Featherhawk. Yes, I got married."

Not that it's done me a lot of good. My husband is off in the boonies somewhere trying to get up enough nerve to come home and live with me! And just when I've heard the most important news of our marriage, I can't even share it.

She stuffed down the angry little voice and responded to the rush of questions.

Edna set a glass of ice water down in front of Clarissa, waited with one eyebrow raised until she took a sip, then picked up her purse and headed for the door.

"Sorry to have bothered you, Clarissa, but truth to tell, I'm plain tuckered," she called. "You go home and relax right at eight. I'll manage without that monster tomorrow. I did it for thirty years."

"Don't worry, Edna. It'll be working in a few minutes. Kyle is a genius when it comes to this stuff." She waved her hand and watched the other woman walk out, then took a deep breath and swivelled her chair around to face the screen once more. "Yes, I'm here. Okay, I can try that."

By the time the familiar library logo was in the upper right hand corner of the screen, Clarissa was starving.

"Yes, that's done it. Thanks, Kyle. Yes, I'll run it tonight just to be sure I didn't lose anything." She listened as he explained how to lock out any changes Edna might inadvertently make to the operating system. "I'll do that right away." A few keystrokes accomplished the task.

Her heart drooped a little at the next question.

"Wade? Oh, he's very good looking. Dark, tall, muscular. He builds things, beautiful things. I've never seen anyone who can transform a place the way he can." She swallowed a lump in her throat as she remembered his whittling at the lake during their family vacation.

Kyle's curious voice brought her back to reality.

"Yes, he's guardian of his sister's four children. That really fills up the old house." She nodded, eyes misty as she thought about the kids. "I love it. They make the place come alive. It's what I've always wanted." She laughed. "Yes, Wade is what I wanted, too. He's the best thing that ever happened to me.

"No, I'll stay here another half hour or so," she murmured, brushing the tears away from the corners of her eyes. "Till closing time. I can run the diagnostics while I wait. Thanks, Kyle. Yes, I'll be sure to tell Wade he's a lucky man. Uh-huh. Bye."

A lucky man? She almost laughed. So lucky, he was going to have to put his dreams, his plans, his future on hold. How lucky was that?

Clarissa pushed it all away and set to work keying in the loans for the day. Her fingers flew over the keys as she forced her concentration to remain on the screen. She had just finished her entries when a huge sheaf of red roses appeared in front of her eyes.

"Oh, my!" The scent of the flowers was overwhelming. Clarissa stood up, trying to straighten her vision and put out her hand to keep from falling. "Oh, my," she breathed, as her stomach rolled, her knees collapsed and she tumbled backward into mind-numbing blackness.

"Clarissa? Oh, God, what have I done wrong now?" Wade gathered the delicately boned body in his arms and carried her over to the thick plush rug in the story-time section. Gently he laid her out on it, then picked up a nearby book and fanned it back and forth above her face to create a breeze in the nearly airless room.

"Please, Clara, don't do this. I'm totally useless with fainting women. I have no idea how to make you wake up. Clara, I love you. That's what I came to say. I wanted to court you, to do it the old-fashioned way. I wanted to make you feel special, loved. To make up for all the things you missed." He dropped the book and picked up her hand.

"I know about love now, Clara. I finally figured it out. I don't know exactly when it happened, I just know that you are the most precious thing in the world to me and I'm never going away without you again. Clarissa?"

Wade searched her face frantically for some sign that she heard and understood what he'd said. But her eyes remained closed, her transparent eyelids tinged with faint blue lines that hid the sparkle of fun he knew was cloaked in their depths.

"Oh, God, please give me another chance. I've messed up so many times. Now I've gone and waited too long, missed another chance to tell someone I love how much she means to me. I can't repeat that mistake again. Not with Clarissa."

He prayed desperately, his mind sending heaven-ward the words he couldn't begin to utter as he searched her face for some sign of life. "Come on, sweetheart. Please wake up. Oh, man! Now I make even my own wife faint."

He cupped the smooth skin of her cheek in one palm, tenderly caressing the curve of her lips, the stubborn lift of her chin, the tiny scar from so long ago.

"Clarissa darling, please don't do this. You're making me very nervous." He gathered her into his arms, pressed his lips against the coil of hair that was even now tumbling across his shoulder. "I love you Clarissa. You said you loved me. Please say it again."

Was that a smile on her lips? Wade leaned closer, felt the puff of air against his skin as she took a deep breath.

"Clarissa? Sweetheart, can you hear me?"

"I can hear something," she whispered, her voice bewildered, bemused. "Say it again, please."

"Say what? Blast it, if I didn't love you so much I'd be yelling right now! Wake up, will you? Please?" He wanted to squeeze her so tight, hold her so close that she'd never go away again. "Please?" he begged, his voice hoarse with worry. It wasn't normal for anyone to be out this long, was it?

The fist that held his heart in its grip loosened just a fraction as her gorgeous eyes blinked open.

"Oh, hi Wade. I just had the most wonderful dream." Clarissa squinted up at him. "You're back," she murmured, fidgeting just a little in his tight hold.

Wade refused to let her go. "Yeah, I'm back. I had it all planned out. I was going to show up here with those flowers, take you out for dinner and tell you how much I love you." He frowned at the drooping roses that lay strewn across her desk. Messed up again!

"You were?" She frowned up at him, ceasing her

movements when his hand tightened around her shoulder.

"Oh."

"Oh? That's all you're gonna say?" He glared at her, furious that all his careful planning was for nothing. This moldy old library was the least romantic place and he'd wanted something special for her, something really exceptional for this woman who'd wrapped her life around his and loved him so tenderly.

"I love you!"

"But—" She studied his face, her hand lifting to brush a lock of hair off his face. "I thought you weren't the type. You said you weren't a family kind of man."

"Yeah, well, what do I know?" He smiled, just to show he wasn't mad at her. "I guess I'm not a regular kind of family man. But then, heaven knows we're not a regular kind of family." He brushed his hand across her forehead. "Are you really all right? I've never been so scared in my life. You went down like a ton of bricks. I thought for sure I'd waited too long again."

"Again?"

Her eyes told him nothing. Her demeanor was the familiar watch-and-see attitude. Wade found himself wishing, no hoping, for some flicker that would tell him she still loved him.

"Yeah, again. I've always waited until it was too late to tell the people I care about how much I love them. I missed my opportunity with my mother and again with Kendra. I sure didn't intend to let it happen a third time."

"Well, go ahead and tell me then."

He blinked at the acerbic tone in her usually soft voice. "I'm not just saying it, Clara. I really do understand what love is. And I know that I love you. I'm not very good at it yet, but I can learn. See—" he checked to be sure she was listening "—it's different this time."

"It is?" She sounded as if she were withdrawing from him.

Wade hurried to explain. "Yeah, it is. This time I'm not running away. Not from anything. No matter what. This time I want to hang around and find out all about love."

"Why?"

"Why?" He swallowed. "What do you mean, why? Because I love you and I love the kids. Because you need me as much as I need you."

"Oh, Wade!" She burst into tears, wrenching herself out of his arms and pushing to her feet.

Wade grabbed her arm when she wobbled a bit, but she pushed him back, balancing one hand on a chair for stability.

"I don't want you to stay with me because I need you. I don't want a husband who thinks I'm a millstone, a burden, somebody who has to be looked after." Tears streamed down her cheeks and dripped onto her not-so-perfectly-pressed blouse. "I don't want to add to your responsibilities!"

He ignored her outstretched hand and gathered her into his arms, tenderly cradling her head against his chest. "But you are a burden, a very special burden! Don't you see, Clarissa. That's what love is all about.

I *want* the privilege and the responsibility of taking care of you and the kids. I want us to share them.''

She stepped back out of the circle of his arms. "You wouldn't say that," she mumbled, turning away. "Not if you knew."

"Knew what?" He turned her around and tipped up her chin so he could look into her eyes, see the truth for himself. Had she changed her mind? Didn't she love him anymore? Had he spoiled that, too? "Clarissa, what's wrong? Are you ill? Is that it? Something serious?"

She nodded slowly, her head jerked up and down twice. "Something very serious." She gulped.

Wade closed his eyes as the knowledge pierced his heart. Oh, God, why had it taken him so long to see the truth? Why had he fought it? How long did they have?

"Wade?"

He opened his eyes.

"I'm pregnant." She stood there, tiny and frail, her eyes huge in that pale oval face that made him catch his breath as her words hit home.

"Pregnant?" His heart burst into a melody of praise. He grabbed her and whirled her around, then stopped when her face went a strange shade of green. "Sorry, darling. Pregnant with a baby? My baby?"

She rolled her eyes. "Yes, of course with a baby."

Funny, she didn't look that happy. Clarissa loved kids. She'd prayed for a baby of her own. Jared had heard her. Why wasn't she happy? Didn't she want to have *his* baby?

"What's wrong? Don't you want to be pregnant?" It cost him dearly to ask that question. He couldn't fathom her not wanting their child, couldn't imagine what he'd do if she rejected them both. At the stunned expression on her face, Wade had his answer. "Okay, you want this baby. So?"

"Babies," she whispered. "It's babies. Two of them. Twins."

Wade sat down. Hard. In the big oak rocking chair he'd seen her use for story time. He swallowed.

Two babies. His tiny little wife, delicate, fragile Clara, was going to have *two* babies? No wonder she'd passed out! He felt a little faint himself.

Clarissa knelt in front of him, her eyes brimming with unshed tears as a stream of worry poured out from her lips.

"You see? That's what I was trying to say. You said you wanted to share the kids, but this will make it six! It's far too much, far beyond the responsibility you ever expected. You'll want to run away every weekend. The house will be so crowded. And what will we do for money? The kids won't want to share the place with a baby. You'll have to take over when I get too tired, and I will get tired, Wade. I already am. Then there's your degree. You won't be able to get to college for years and years all because of me. I'll weigh you down and make you sorry—"

Wade laid a finger across her lips, stopping the litany of protests that she was rattling off. "Come here, Clarissa. You and I need to get some things straightened out." He pulled her closer, then down onto his lap. His arms tenderly cradled her against his chest as held the most precious thing in his life.

"Listen, sweetheart, above all else, I love you. Got that?"

She nodded slowly, eyes dark and troubled. "Yes, but…"

"No buts. I love you. Do you love me?" He waited only a moment for her nod, then heaved a sigh of relief. "Thank you, God! Okay, then, nothing else really matters, does it?"

"Yes, Wade it does. We have to figure out how we'll manage. It's going to be such a strain on you."

"No, it won't," he told her firmly. "It will be a delight and a pleasure every time I look at you and see those children growing inside you. Every time I hold one of our children, I'll know they are a special gift from God, just as you are. And I'll thank Him every day for permitting me to have another chance at love."

She frowned, unwilling to believe. "But it's not what you wanted. You wanted to be free."

"Did I?" Wade smiled, threading his fingers through the long shiny strands of silver-gilt hair. "I think I wanted to be exactly where I am. I just didn't know it. You see, honey, I spent a lot of years trying to avoid responsibility because I didn't think I could live up to the demands of having someone love me." Wade checked to be sure she was hearing him.

"Sometimes when you feel boxed in, you make up a dream so you have a reason to get out. Going to college, becoming an architect, that was my dream. It got me off the reservation, got me my high school credits, and gave me something to focus on when things got pretty rough after I left home."

"And now you'll never get that dream," she moaned. "Two more children mean we can't afford for you to go back to school, Wade. I've ruined that.''

He pulled her tight against his chest and held her for a long minute. "No, my darling wife, you have given me the most precious gifts I can ever imagine. As it happens, I don't want to go to college. I don't want to become an architect. I like my life just the way it is."

Clarissa's voice rumbled against his chest, but the words were clear. "You're just saying that, trying to make me feel better for spoiling things."

"Honey, God is in control. Isn't that what you're always saying?" He tugged her head back and winked at her, his eyes daring her to answer back. He laid his palm very carefully on her flat tummy. "These babies are ours, something we will share with each other for the rest of our lives. I love them already because they'll bring us closer."

Her stare never wavered. "Are you sure?"

Wade nodded. "You wondered why I had to go away, didn't you?" She raised her eyebrows, her lips refusing to admit it. He grinned. "I know you did, Clara. Well, the truth is, I'd begun to realize that what I really wanted from life wasn't what I thought it was. I wanted to love you, I wanted us to be together in a real marriage and I wanted to tell you that, but I didn't know how because I was all mixed up."

"And it's straight now?" She looked dubious.

"I think so. You see, what I've always wanted more than anything is respectability. Pastor Mike pointed out to me that I liked having people comment on my lovely wife, our great kids, our happy home.

And he was right. I did, I do. For once I wasn't the outcast, the poor dumb Indian who couldn't do things right. For once, I was the envy of other people. You gave me that and I loved it.''

He grinned at her, hoping to ease the strain he could feel still holding her slender body in its grip.

''You made that possible, Clara. You. Your stalwart defense of me, your steady support and unwavering decision to pull your weight, to give me enough freedom to figure things out, made me realize that I was letting you do all the work and I was gaining all the benefit. I didn't want other people to think I was a great architect, a wonderful builder—I wanted you to think I was the greatest thing since sliced bread.''

''I do,'' she assured him softly, her eyes downcast, reddened cheeks telling him she was embarrassed by the wealth of feeling that burst out in those words.

''I know.'' He kissed the tip of her nose. ''So I figured if I worked my tail off proving myself, I wouldn't have to say the words. That you'd understand how much I cared.''

''I didn't know,'' she whispered, the ache in her voice audible. ''I wish I had.''

''That's what finally drove it home. I was wimping out, hoping I wouldn't have to actually say the words and hang myself out on a limb.'' He shook his head. ''Stupid!''

''Wade, I don't understand.'' She needed reassurance and Wade gave it to her.

''I didn't want to be rejected. I didn't want to take the chance that once you found out how selfish I'd been, you'd realize I'm to blame for Kendra's death and that I should never have been given the privilege of caring for her children. Kendra died because I was too self-absorbed to be her big brother. I failed her miserably. What's to show you I won't do it again?"

He sighed. "That's why I've always run away. I'm a chicken, Clara. A selfish chicken who disappoints even himself. I want to bask in the glory without giving up anything. Even for my own sister. How much worse could I get with you?"

She took his hand. "You *were* her big brother, Wade, and you protected her the best you could. She loved you. Besides, even then God was in control. If He'd wanted her alive, Kendra would be here now." Her eyes were swimming with emotion. "He was in charge, not you. And He makes beauty come from sadness. Beauty like our family."

Wade closed his eyes, drew in a ragged breath of relief and told her the truth.

"Do you know what drew me back to you? I figured that if I can't manage the whole thing, can't be man enough to accept your love and love you back the way God loves us, then I couldn't keep accepting your love. That scared me so badly. I've finally realized that love is an all-or-nothing proposition, that it's a two-way deal." He cupped her face in his hands.

"I need your love, Clarissa. It makes me stronger, more complete. Without your love I'm just running away from life, from everything I've wanted for so long. I want to come home, Clarissa. I want to stand by your side and watch the kids grow, see the babies born, celebrate Christmas and New Year's in that big ol' house."

"It's going to be a lot of work," she warned, but

her eyes sent a shaft of warmth straight to his heart. "It's not going to be easy."

"Running away is easy," he whispered. "But loving you is the most precious job I could ever have. Please tell me I'm not fired."

Clarissa's eyes roved over his face. He had the feeling she was imprinting the memory deep within. When her arms whispered around his neck, he let out the breath he didn't realize he'd been holding.

"You're not fired, husband," she whispered in his ear. "In fact, you've just received a promotion to father-to-be. Congratulations."

The sound of shoe leather tap-tapping over the marble floor drew Wade's attention from Clarissa's kissable mouth. He craned his neck to see two elderly ladies peering first at the wilting roses, then at them. Their faces bloomed with curiosity.

"I'm sorry, ladies," he announced, his arms tightening around Clarissa, "the library is closed early today. My wife and I are celebrating."

Epilogue

"**W**hat is that awful smell?" Wade's voice rumbled from the depths of the satin quilt he'd dragged over his head the last time the babies' cries told him they needed changing.

"I don't know." Clarissa sat up, yawned and sniffed. She wrinkled her nose in distaste. "Should I go check?"

He lifted the quilt and peered one eye out at her. "Why? Can you make it go away?"

"I doubt it. It seems pretty strong." She giggled when his hand snaked around her neck and he tugged her head down for a quick kiss under her grandmother's hand-stitched quilt. "That isn't going to get rid of it, either," she laughed, kissing him back.

"Maybe not, but I sure feel better."

They both jumped as the bedroom door slammed open and four hearty voices joined together in a rousing rendition of "Happy Mother's Day to you."

"Déjà vu," Wade whispered in her ear. But he

emerged just enough to lean against the headboard and watch as Tildy presented his wife with a breakfast tray. "It's a good thing you're not pregnant," he teased, eyeing the glistening fish eye that gleamed out of a blackened body. "What is it, Tildy?"

"Kippers, of course. I ordered them in especially for today because Clarissa likes fish." The girl chewed her lip, her self-doubt obvious. "Did I cook them okay?"

From the next room, the babies made their presence known and the boys hurried out to collect the squalling infants. They returned, Jared with Kendra Lane, and Pierce with Andrew Lane.

Clarissa couldn't stop the tears that bubbled up from the fountain of happiness inside. They squeezed out from her eyes and tumbled down her cheeks as she surveyed the seven members of her precious God-given family.

"You did everything just right," she whispered, her heart overflowing with heavenly thanks.

Wade's arm curved around her shoulder, his lips gentle on her hair as he held out a small flat parcel covered in red hearts.

"Happy Mother's Day, sweetheart."

Clarissa searched, but couldn't read his eyes. All she could see was an overflowing love there, a quiet gentle love that told her he thought himself the luckiest man alive. She waited until he'd removed the breakfast tray, then slid a finger under the tape holding the triangular folds in place.

"I don't need anything, Wade," she mumbled, embarrassed by her abundance of tears. "I already have it all."

"Now you do," he whispered smugly as he watched the shock spread over her face. "Now you most certainly do."

"It's a miracle." Clarissa stared at the official legal document granting full and complete adoption of the children Tildy, Lacey, Jared and Pierce to Mr. Wade and Mrs. Clarissa Featherhawk.

"A Mother's Day miracle," Wade agreed. His finger scooped up her tear and kissed it. "For the most deserving mother God could have found us. We love you, Mom."

Clarissa clutched the document to her chest and held on for the sheer joy of it. "Come here you guys," she laughed as the kids tucked a baby into each of Wade's arms, then collapsed onto the bed around her in a group hug. Her eyes met his over the tumble of heads. "Each of you are my very own, personal, heaven-sent miracles. I love you so much."

Wade's earsplitting grin told her the feeling was mutual.

*   *   *   *   *

Watch for Blair's romance,
HIS ANSWERED PRAYER,
the next book in Lois Richer's
IF WISHES WERE WEDDINGS *miniseries,*
coming only to Love Inspired
in October 2000.

Dear Reader,

Thanks for picking up my latest book. I've had so much fun writing about Clarissa and Wade, and their four charges. Isn't it funny how God works? We pray and pray for something, He gives it to us and then we wonder if we can handle it!

In this story Clarissa thought her heart's desire was a husband and a baby. What she really wanted, what we all long for, is unconditional love. We yearn for somebody who will take us, warts and all, and hold us close on the bad hair days, on the cranky days, on the days when nothing seems to go right. Sometimes we can find love in another person, but true unconditional love comes from the Father. He wants us to seek His help, just as much as a mother wants her child to come to her when he hurts. We may think we're a nuisance, but not to Him. He thinks we're His beautiful children and He loves us.

I wish you great rewards as you start each new day with Him in mind.

Blessings,